Tales Eve - An Anthology of short stories

I0571174

Evincepub
Publishing

Evincepub Publishing

Parijat Extension, Bilaspur, Chhattisgarh 495001
First Published by Evincepub Publishing 2018
Copyright © Charles E. Ekka 2018
All Rights Reserved.
ISBN: 978-93-87063-15-0
Price: Rs.300/-

Tales Eve

An Anthology of short stories

By
Charles E. Ekka

About The Book

The short stories in the book are complete work of fiction and it is the first book by author Charles E. Ekka. Each story dwells with its respective main characters that take place during the time of middle ages to eighteen and nineteenth century world and each story is complex with different genre that include adventure, fantasy, mystery, horror and romance with dark and humble theme.

About The Author

Charles E. Ekka is a final year graduate student and this is his first fiction Anthology book. In mid years of high school, he learned about book publishing and got interested in it and only after high school he began to write his first few books which had no proper theme and never got its ending. And so on, during the forthcoming days, his interest of writing stories had almost fainted but somehow he again got interested in writing stories and after some hard thoughts and imagination, he wrote this first few short stories as an Anthology.

Contents

The Decision of Daniel Ewart

1. The Decision of Daniel Ewart

It was the arrival of cold winter evenings and there was no one who looked at that little boy, sitting beside the street. His name was Daniel Ewart. He was a nine years old orphan and was homeless for five months. He doesn't know who his father was but his mother died after his birth. He was raised by his aunt, his mother's older sister. She herself had seven children, excluding him and they were harsh on him, though they sent him to school for least three years, where he learnt to read and write.

She always gave him works which he was too young to do it, like washing clothes for the entire family members, cleaning the floor and get scolded for small reasons, like missing little dust on the floor while cleaning and her own children bullied him, always. He wanted to run away but fear of dying in hunger locked him inside his aunt's house. Then one day her aunt kicked him out for breaking a flower vase and that's how he became homeless. He somehow survived by eating whatever he could find in the garbage and with someone's pity, he would get a piece of bread and walk away. But the warm days and nights were turning cold and he didn't have any warm clothes to resist it. He again survived for one week without a roof, shivering but as the time passed the cold was giving him more trouble.

One evening, it was very cold than the rest of the past evening and he was shivering and no one bothered to look at him which was not a new thing or bothered to be. Then the church bells ranged which was neither a new thing but that moment Daniel felt like he was going to die and he became angry to himself that what was his mistake that he had to suffer so miserable. As he was going to sob, someone covered him with a warm blanket and the church bells stopped ringing. He turned to see, who the person was? It was an old beggar. He had been seeing the little boy for almost three months while he was begging around. He knew by his experienced long life instinct that the boy had been kicked out from his relative house and he was an orphan. He didn't bother whether he live or die. But for some weeks he saw him shivering out in cold and that moment also he didn't felt to bother about him, until now.

Daniel stood up; holding the blanket covered his body from neck to bottom. It was warm and he caught it tight. He looked up to the wrinkled face of the old man with white beards and his long court with stitched from several parts with different colour clothes.

"My name is Wilson, what is yours?" asked the old beggar, simply. But Daniel didn't reply.

"My name is Wilson and what is your name little rat?" he asked again, but still no answer. "Do you have your tongue boy?" little harshly.

"Oh, yes, yes I do. My name is Daniel Ewart", finally answered the boy.

"Okay, Daniel can you walk, by using your two little legs. Do you have two legs?"

"Yes, yes I have."

"Come follow me and if you stop, I'll take the blanket and leave you out here in cold", declared Wilson, picking his sack bag and walked by him.

Daniel followed him because he doesn't have any other option. They kept on walking until they reached the town wall gates and walked out to the meadows and he took him somewhere into the forest and brought Daniel to a hut which he was his home.

"Make yourself home and if you don't like it, you can leave, anytime", said Wilson.

The hut had one room and the walls were made of wood and had tiny holes from where one can look through inside and out and the roof was thatched. The old beggar used a bundle of hay as his bed and pillow which he collected from a nearby farm and the farmer gave him, showing him pity. He also shared some hay with the boy so that he could rest and then he himself went to sleep without opening his boots or jacket. The hay bed was not comfortable for Daniel as the bed of his aunt's house but good enough from the street and to keep him away from getting killed by cold.

Next morning, Wilson opened a secret closet which was below his hay bed, an underground hole, covered by a big wooden lap pieces. It was his treasure pot. It was built naturally a long time ago and was shaped rectangular and one adult person can fit in till his waist. Wilson had made the hole little adjustable by his own hands and used it to collect shoes and clothes which he found in the trash or given by someone but none of them was stolen. He gave a pair of shoes, one brown and one black to Daniel as he was bare footed. It didn't fit him perfect but he managed it. Then they went to the town to beg and they continued begging together in coming few days. And so before the first snowfall, they had collected enough food for both to survive the winter.

The winter arrived and passed and by the arrival of spring, they continued going to the town as usual and begged and whatever they collect they would share and eat. By then the boy had adjusted himself and was comfortable with his new life, which Wilson clearly observed it. But soon Wilson realised that he was wasting the young boy's strength in false practice. He knew he was old and cannot do any hard labour so he was devoted to begging but Daniel was too young. He had a future to learn, more about work and earn of his own.

And so on the following day, he took the boy to an inn called Trotter's Inn Service which was owned by Trotter family, who were total four family members, mother, father and two sons- who were the same age as Daniel. The Trotter's Inn was few miles away from the outskirts of the cross-state and two and half hour away from the town gate. Many travellers which include mostly traders and merchants cross by and usually most of the time, they visit to eat, drink and rest, as it was the only inn comes by road and it was a very good business for Trotter family, who were doing business for past five generation.

There was a time when Wilson used to come and beg at the Trotters and they give him a piece of bread and that's how he knows them. Wilson talked with Mr. Trotter who was the head of the family and the inn. He understood the situation and agreed to hire Daniel as his employ. He discussed that in return as his income he would get two loaves of bread and two pounds for his everyday work. Daniel hesitated because it was the same work which he used to do when he was at his aunt's house and got scared. After insisting several times by Wilson, he agreed but not on his own will. On his first day of work, he was given to collect the used dishes of customers and bringing them to the kitchen basin, where Larry and Lewis the sons of the Trotter couple, washed them. He did well and still, he was scared.

That same noon, a customer sitting by the table moved his hand while talking, that accidently bumped on Daniel's face. He was holding a lot of dishes and mugs and he fell.

"Oh, I apologise", said the customer, and moved from his seat and picked him. "Are you okay boy?"

Mr. Trotter heard the sound of falling of dishes and came.

"My apologies, it was my mistake, I bumped onto your employ", said the customer. Then Mrs. Trotter came after serving two customers.

"Daniel, are you okay? Are you hurt?", she asked, worried.

He looked to her. "No", he replied.

"Seemed like everything is fine", concluded Mr. Trotter.

The customer sat back on the seat while Lewis came and helped to pick up the dishes and they took it to the basin.

"Am I going to get punished by your father?" Daniel asked Lewis.

Lewis felt awkward, not aware of his past. "Why would you be punished?", he replied.

"I just, I just dropped the dishes", he said.

"No, and it wasn't your mistake", he replied, simply.

Daniel was little amazed because the reason why he was kicked of the house was his aunt actually pushed him and the vase on his hand fell and he was blamed but here it was different. But he still feared that he will be punished if he does any mistake.

He asked Lewis again, "Lewis do your father ever punish or beat you when you do a mistake?"

"No, but only time he scolded me when I arrived home late but he never beat me or my brother. Why do you ask that?"

"Just... making sure of my safety", replied Daniel.

"Don't worry brother, no one is going to hurt you here just try not to repeat the mistake", he explained.

Daniel felt relief that they are no danger to him and only have to make sure not to repeat the same mistake. In the noon, the entire family member gathered for lunch. They all sat around a table, including Daniel and they each got a slice of pie, curry and bread. It was the most delicious food that he had eaten in his entire life.

"Do you want more Larry", asked Mr. Trotter, holding the pot of curry.

"No", he replied.

"Lewis."

"No."

"Daniel."

"No wait yes, I want a little", he replied.

Mr. Trotter fetched him the curry and Daniel felt nice and it was the first time, he received a generous response by someone, other than Wilson.

"Come on boys get to work, five customers arrived", exclaimed Mrs. Trotter and they moved and so Daniel, leaving his unfinished lunch but he was stopped by Mrs. Trotter and insisted on finishing his lunch first and then coming to work.

Daniel did as Mrs. Trotter told him and then got back to work. So, the first day of his work was complete. He was given two loafs and paid two pounds by Mr. Trotter as for the agreement.

As he was about to leave, Lewis and Larry came running, holding wooden swords and Larry asked, "Hey Daniel want to play sword fight with us?"

"I can't, I have to go now and give Wilson this food", he replied.

"Okay but are you coming tomorrow, right, we will play tomorrow", said Lewis.

Daniel couldn't decide what to say but he replied, "I'll try".

He returned to the hut. After a while, Wilson also returned from the town but this time he was mugged by two people and the money he had collected were taken and the food was wasted, during the struggle. However, he does not have to sleep hungry. Daniel had earned from his day work. He gave him one and he ate it, quietly.

"Hmmm... sweet", he said.

"Mr. Trotter gave me", replied Daniel, "and I was thinking of working there for few more days."

"Do whatever you like, little rat but don't do anything wrong", he replied.

He drank some water and went to sleep. He lies on his hay bed and gazed up to the thatched roof and thought about the morning activities. The family seemed nice and decided going back to work under them. So on the following day, he continued working in Trotter's Inn and in the coming years, Daniel got totally along with the family. The Trotters treat him very nicely; like a family member that his past bruises were healed that he faced as a child. But one tragedy happened. Wilson the old beggar died when it was five years since he joined the Trotter's Inn. He was very upset about losing him but he moved on.

As Daniel grew tall, Trotters taught him cooking, fishing and riding a horse and also how to use a sword and wrestling. The first Trotter who started the inn business was first a sword trainer and a wrestler and it was his profession but the training classes didn't pay him enough for him and his family of nine members, including him, six daughters, one son and wife. So he started the inn business which was now passed to present successor and so the sword and wrestling lessons. And by some little luck Daniel got a chance to learn it. They also bought him a steel sword and a leather belt carrier with a scabbard to carry the sword like their sons which he always kept with him, except during the work and soon after a lot of training during free times, he became an expert in both the fighting arts with no fear. Fifteen years passed since he first came to work and now he was twenty-four whereas the two son of Mr. Trotter, Larry the older one was twenty-five and Lewis the younger one was twenty-four.

"Lewis! Lewis!" cried Mrs. Trotter, standing in the backyard of the inn. It was evening and the last customers had left and more to come sooner or later. "Oh dear, where is this lazy boy? Lewis!"

Meantime Daniel finished cleaning the dishes used by customers with Larry.

"Mr. Trotter, I'm done with my work shift. I'm leaving now", said Daniel and took off his apron and placed it on the hanger and picked his sword.

"See you tomorrow, Daniel", said Larry and went up to his room to rest.

"Okay, see you tomorrow", he replied.

"Take you income", reminded Mr. Trotter.

Daniel took his income and came out of the inn through the back door and found Mrs. Trotter.

"Oh, it's you, Daniel. I thought Lewis", said Mrs. Trotter. "Is Lewis inside?"

"Lewis... Lewis is not in the inn, Mrs. Trotter", replied Daniel.

"What? Lewis is not here?" She was little surprised. "But a moment ago I thought he was outside."

"He isn't here."

"So where is he?", asked Mrs. Trotter.

"I don't know. He only said that he will be back in a moment. Okay, I'm leaving Mrs. Trotter."

"Daniel wait...", she interrupted.

"What is it, Mrs. Trotter?" he asked.

"I want you to go to the town with Larry and get the inn's groceries. It is also getting late", she requested.

"Okay I will", he agreed, nodding.

She gave him the list and a purse full of the amount to Larry. He was almost asleep in his bed but he moved as it was for the family business. Then they went to the town on the horse cart.

"Did my brother gave you any details about where he is?" asked Larry on the way going to the grocery shop.

"No, he didn't? What do you think, where could he be gone during work?"

"No idea but he has been acting strange for a couple of weeks".

"Strange? Like what?"

"Like smiling alone and when I ask him he says nothing", he replied.

They reached the store and they asked the daughter of Mr. Watson. She was the in-charge of the store and she told them that her father was sick and so he couldn't deliver the groceries and she also failed to deliver it to them, because two of the person who worked for them was on vacation. But it was good that they arrived. They loaded the grocery on their cart, paid the full amount to her and started to ride back. As they came out of the town passed the meadows, foothills, and arrived at the beginning of forest road they saw a couple below a tree. Larry was going to ignore them but then he recognized that person. It was none other than his brother Lewis, skipping from his work.

"Lewis", he said, he was determined.

"Where?", said Daniel and turned to that direction, he was facing.

The couple noticed them and Lewis got terrified that he was busted. He excused from the girl and she went away and he walked to them and Larry stopped the cart. Lewis sat on the cart without speaking anything while Larry was turning red for leaving the work. They remained silent for few seconds.

"Who was that pretty girl?", Daniel asked Lewis.

"Pretty girl... oh yes she is pretty", replied Lewis, "her name is Rachael and she lives at a nearby farm and I know her for a month... And I'm really, really sorry that you have to do my part of work."

"Do you know what, I was almost asleep", said Larry in angry mood.

But he got no answer. They remained silent again, after covering the more than half distance on the forest road and then Lewis said, "So boys, will you do me a favour. Please don't tell to father and mother that I was hanging out with… you know what."

"Twenty pounds and I saw nothing", blackmailed Larry.

"What twenty pounds? That is more than the earning of mine in the family business. You cannot demand that much. Have some mercy. From where am I going to get that much." looking to Daniel, "And you must be thinking the same. Please don't."

"Don't worry, I'm not into this."

"Well you can give me from the treasure box of yours, which is in your wardrobe, locked", reminded Larry.

"Treasure box? Hey when did you learnt about that?" he replied, astonished, "Did you took my future saving?" voice turned little harshly.

"No, I didn't. I'm not a thief and everyone knows about it."

"I don't know anything about your treasure box", interrupted Daniel.

"Okay fine", said Larry. "I only know about it and if you want me to keep my mouth shut then you have to pay for it."

"No, I won't, go and tell mother and father. I'm not giving you my money. It's my investments for my future. And it is hard work."

"Investment for your future?", said Daniel. "Are you collecting it for your marriage?"

"No, it's not only about marriage", answered Lewis, "it's about living after marriage too."

"What do you mean?" asked Daniel.

"Means… if not… okay, let us just take the example our inn. The business of our inn is shining only because our father is the only son of my grandfather, so he got it by birth and then we came, Larry and I and here comes the misery. If some day Lewis and I get married and have two-two or may be three-three children and all of them are boys. Then our Inn business won't be enough to hold them and then they get married and so… there gone be chaos that who would be the next owner of the inn."

"So now you can predict the future", protested Larry.

"Seriously for God's sake, explain what would be the solution if that would happen", replied Lewis.

"Whatever", ignored Larry and they reached the inn.

After getting the grocery into the storage, Daniel returned home, the hut. In the past years, he had made many improvements with his savings and was more comfortable than before. The walls were properly nailed with fine wood and had no tiny holes as it was before, the roof got a chimney with a small fireplace but it still had one room with a proper bed and some warm clothes inside a small trunk.

He took off his sword belt and suspended over a nail on the wall, lighted the lantern and lie on his bed, gazing the roof. He thought about what Lewis spoke to them, early this evening. He considered that Lewis's plan for his future was not bad. It was a brilliant idea. He assumed if Lewis marry that girl named Rachael and then Larry gets married to someone and have children and they all get into the inn business and in the coming age, all of them will become old and so does he. He could end of like Wilson. And that thought scared Daniel. Then he decided to do something else for his future.

The next day Daniel went to work as usual and also thought what he could do other than cleaning and cooking. He kept on thinking, alongside doing his work. He thought for a moment of opening an inn just like Trotters, but it would take a lot of money to build it. If he had thought like Lewis earlier, then that would be quite a benefit to him and besides talking loan from money lender was a very bad idea, if cannot repay the full debt. And other works like farming or opening a grocery store had the same risk. Many days past but he could come to any decision for his future plan and if came the assumption always ends up in tragedy. Then one night as he was thinking he fell asleep. He dreamed of someone knocking at his door. But as the knock became louder he woke up and learnt that his door was actually been knocked. Who could be at this time? He thought. He rose up from his bed and took the lantern in his hand. The door kept on knocking.

"Who is there?" he asked.

"Help me please", somebody responded. "Help me."

Daniel got alert and he placed the lantern beside the door and took his sword on his hand and opened the door slightly and was startled after finding that it was a little girl, sobbing. He opened the door completely and bent to his knees and asked, "What happened? What are you doing here?"

"Please help me. I'm lost", requested the little girl. Daniel gazed out if someone was behind her, but no one was there.

"Come inside", he said.

Daniel gave her his warm blanket. She was shivering from the night cold.

"Are you thirsty?" He asked.

She nodded and he fetched her water. Then he gave her a loaf of bread on a plate.

"Eat this, you must be hungry", he said and she quickly grabbed that bread and ate it as she was starving.

"What is your name?" he asked politely, "and my name is Daniel."

She paused and then swallowed a bit.

"Evelyn", she answered.

"So Evelyn, did you ran away from your house?"

"No, I was returning with my guard from Lord Caster's party. In the middle of the way my horse went crazy and took me into the forest and I got lost."

"Wait you mentioned Lord... right", and she nodded. "So are you belonging to some kind of noble family?"

"Yes, I'm a Princess, daughter of King Alister", she declared.

Hearing that she is a Princess, Daniel was stunned. What the hell am I hearing? He thought. She was exhausted and her eyes were getting closed. Daniel looked around and found his own bed would be more suitable for her. He cleaned the bed dust and took every single care that he could give her. She slept on the bed and he slept on the floor.

Next morning, when she woke up, he took her to the Trotters and explained everything to the couple and she was given breakfast.

"So what are we going to do now?" asked Mrs. Trotter to her husband.

"The Royal soldier must be preparing or could have started the search for her, by now and sooner or later they will arrive here for sure", concluded Mr. Trotter.

"Till then we should keep her safe."

"It is a miracle that she managed to arrive at your doors", said Mrs. Trotter.

"Yes it is and where are Larry and Lewis?" asked Daniel.

"They have gone to get groceries", answered Mrs. Trotter.

After finishing her breakfast Evelyn came to them.

"Please take me home", she demanded.

"Oh Your Majesty, I suggest you please wait for a little longer, wait until your Royal guards arrive. They will come in search of you and when they will arrive, they will take you home, safely", insisted Mr. Trotter, politely. "And if my sons arrive first then they will take you home."

"I want to go home, now", she demanded."Please take me home."

They looked to each other. If anything happens to her, they could be in trouble.

"Okay, I'll take her", decided Daniel.

"How? We don't even have a spare horse", reminded Mrs. Trotter.

"I will carry her on my back, way to the palace."

Daniel checked his sword and carried her on his back and Mrs. Trotter prayed for their safe journey. He carried her through the forest road and came out to meadows. He took a little rest, under a tree and then again carried her and started to walk. They came across another forest road and walked through. As they were almost out of the forest, a Royal scout of search party arrived from the front. Daniel stopped them and they saw him carrying the Princess on his back. They all were astonished.

"Oh God, it's the Princess", said one of them.

"Princess", said Commander Harrison.

He came down from the horse and she came down from his back.

"Commander Harrison", said Evelyn and ran towards him and hugged.

"Your father and I were so worried about you", said Harrison.

The guards surrounded Daniel and saw he was holding a sword. They thought he was a threat and Daniel felt like they were going to hurt.

"Hey, wait..." said Daniel.

"Shall we arrest him?" asked one of the guards.

"What?" said Daniel, confused.

"You shut up!" interrupted another guard and pushed him down.

"Stop! Don't hurt him! That person saved me", interrupted Evelyn but they didn't listened. They were thinking Daniel was her kidnapper.

"Who gave you orders to touch that man!" exclaimed Harrison and they moved back. "Don't you have ears... when Princess ordered you all to move back? Don't you have any respect of you duty?"

They knelled down and apologized to the Princess and their commander and told that they were thinking he was her kidnapper. Daniel stood up and Harrison went close to him. He was clean shaved, middle age man and had a long golden Christian cross, hung by a silver chain around his neck. He was a pious man and he was the head of the Royal guards.

"What is your name, young man?" he asked, politely.

"It's Daniel, Daniel Ewart, sir" he answered.

"So Mr. Ewart, you need to come with us."

"But I have done nothing wrong. I was helping the Princess."

"He saved me, why are you arresting him?" interrupted Evelyn.

"No, no Princess, you misunderstood. I'm not arresting him", explained Harrison, "he saved you and I and your father would like to reward him."

Daniel was speechless.

"Come", smiling to Daniel, "ride with one of my men."

While riding back to the palace, they passed through the capital city named Zeus. It was huge and beautiful. He heard the church bell ringing and saw that it was bigger than the church of the village and the town. It was a very splendid experience for him which might not happen ever again. King Alister was standing in the hallway and watching down the flowers of the Royal garden, though the window. He was anxious and worried about her daughter when a guard came running and informed him that the Princess had been found and she had returned. He rushed to see her. When both father and daughter saw each other, they ran and hugged.

"Oh thank God, you are okay, I almost thought I lost you", said Alister and his worry ended.

Then Daniel was introduced to the King and Harrison asked some questions about him. And finally, he was given his reward. Two hundred gold coins. He was speechless because it was a very large amount and he had never seen nor had he hold it on his palm. He felt very happy. One of the guards brought him back to the Trotter's inn by riding with him on his horse back and returned.

He told the Trotters everything and about his reward. He wanted to share his reward with them and Larry and Lewis had accepted his offer but their parents interrupted and suggested that he deserved to keep all the reward because he was the person who gave shelter to the Princess and he carried her on his back. Now, one thing was left on Daniel's mind, that what he should do with his reward? He thought that he could spend in something which could be useful for his future just like Lewis had prepared for it and he started thinking again about his future plan.

Three days passed thinking and on the fifth day, two Royal soldiers from the palace arrived at the inn. They entered when Mrs. Trotter was serving the customer and he asked her if Daniel Ewart was still working with them. Daniel was carrying a flour sack to the kitchen when one of the soldiers noticed him and called him outside to talk in private.

"Okay, I'm just keeping the sack", he said.

After keeping the flour sack, he went out to talk with them. Mrs. Trotter wondered what they were talking about. After a few minutes of talk, Daniel came inside and the Royal soldiers returned.

"Excuse me, are you Daniel Ewart?" asked a customer and other also turned to him.

"Yes, that is me."

"So this is Daniel Ewart?" "Oh, he is Daniel Ewart?" "I thought he was a Trotter?" said some customers, amazed, noticing him for the first time.

"Yes, I'm a Ewart not a Trotter, so what?"

"Did you saved the Princess?" asked another customer.

"Yes, he did and he carried her to the palace, almost", said Mrs. Trotter.

"So what's the big deal?" asked Daniel.

"Nothing, I was hearing your names, from everyone's tongue at Zeus", said a customer.

"Even I heard about you but didn't expect to see you", said another.

"We all are", said another. "You have become quite famous and great job by the way."

"Okay everyone, you all saw him, eat your meal and don't forget to pay", said Mrs. Trotter and she took him inside the kitchen.

"Looks like you have become popular", marked Lewis.

"Okay, okay, so Daniel why the Royal guards were here?" she asked.

Daniel explained that the purpose of their visit was that they offered him a job as a Royal guard in the palace which was a very high responsibility and honourable job position in the kingdom. He will be given a rough training and if he passed the training, he will become a Royal guard. If he was interested then he should come by tomorrow noon.

"So what did you tell them?" asked Mr. Trotter.

"Well, I'm not interested", he replied.

"Why would they ask you to be the guard?" questioned Mrs. Trotter.

"When I was in the palace, Harrison the Commander, questioned me and I told them that I know how to use a sword and wrestling and that why they came", answered Daniel.

Mr. Trotter sighed and said, "Okay let's go back to work."

Later in the home, Daniel thought, whether to take the job or not. Lewis will move on if he gets married and so does Larry. If they will be living in joined family, then the inn wouldn't provide enough space for him and beside his skills of cleaning and cooking won't be need any more if the Trotter's daughter-in-laws joins the family. And then he fell asleep.

Next morning as the Trotter family was getting ready to open the inn, Daniel arrived carrying a bag and a role of his blanket. Mr. Trotter saw the stuff and he understood that Daniel had made his decision. He greeted everyone goodbye with a hug and returned the sword which they had gifted him because he will be getting another sword when he will become the Royal guard.

"Come visiting us sometimes or if you face any problem or homeless or hungry, just come anytime and we will be there to open the door for you", said Mrs. Trotter.

She started to sob because Daniel was like her son and she wasn't ready for this moment. Her family hugged her to give her support and Daniel walked towards the palace. He walked through the same way which he used to take the Princess and then walked through the city of Zeus. Till then his name was deemed from everyone's tongue. He reached the palace gate till noon and met Harrison outside the gate.

"I knew you will come", said Harrison, smiling and a person standing beside him wrote his full name and he also amazed that it was Daniel Ewart and he gave him a smile and cheered him.

"Give your best and pass the test", he said and Daniel nodded.

Then Daniel came to know that he wasn't the only one. There were eleven other men who were assigned for the Royal guards. They looked strong, older and two of them were taller than Daniel. Some of them were foot guards before, and some were from Royal army and there was also a hunter. They looked as if one person was worth ten people but neither Daniel had come to give up so easily. They were taken to a camp on the hill where Harrison explained that why they were selected? It was because they had found them trust worth and General Frost of the Royal army was appointed to train them. Frost also came to know about Daniel but he treated like other candidates because he was the person who guards the border of the kingdom and saving the Princess was a past event for him. Other candidates also came to know about him but they didn't care.

One the first day they were lectured about the kingdom's history, enemy and the story of brave ones and then they were given good food and sleep under that one tent. Next morning, their physical strength was checked by running miles, horse riding and swimming. Daniel performed well and came fourth. Then use of tool that was archery, spears and swords was given. Daniel was bad at archery and had no idea how to use it while the others had some experience, even though their aim was not good. Here he got help by a candidate named Joshua; he was a hunter and second best archer among them. He taught him how to hold and aim for the target and by the end of final archery test; Daniel became better and came forth again. He learnt better archery over a month by regular overnight practice. During the two months of training, two of them were disqualified. One broke his leg, after accidently falling from the horse and one hurt his ankle while running. Then wrestling practice and Daniel came second because Mr. Trotter had trained him well.

Joshua was bad at wrestling, so Daniel helped him and gave him some advice and he came third from the last.

There was a tall person and he was better at everything and he was showing off and Frost had a big expectation with him but he was very careless and broke his leg by falling by getting hit by the horse. Then Joshua also left after receiving a letter from his neighbour that his wife was sick and she cannot feed her four years old daughter and requested him to return immediately. Daniel felt very bad for him but Joshua encouraged him not to give up when he was gone. Now eight were left including Daniel and they competed hard and no one was backing off. Four months passed since they began the training and then two more were disqualified and then another two and remained four people including Daniel and the other tall man.

They were taught the manner about how to greet a Royal person and how to address them which they all four passed. Almost eight months since their training, Harrison arrived at the camp and he was introduced to the four guards which he demanded. Harrison looked to Daniel and nodded once and Daniel felt proud on himself. They were given uniforms and a new sword and were all taken to the church, where they signed their full name on a record book on which all the past and present Royal guards name were signed. And then they took an oath by placing their right hand on the Bible that they will protect their masters with full responsibility.

They were declared Royal guards. They congratulated and hugged each other happily and later Harrison posted each of them with a different person where Daniel was chosen to be the guard of Princess Evelyn. He was introduced to everyone at the throne chamber and he bowed and promised that he will do his duty with full responsibility. Evelyn was very happy that it was Daniel and everybody inside the palace came to know about his name again and about him that he was the one who saved the Princess that night. The first day of Daniel as a guard went well; he stood by the Princess most of the time, not a big deal. The dawn fell and the day of the service was over. He was given a personal chamber in which he slept and so a week was going to pass.

And he also started to know almost all the people who work inside the palace and on the fifth day, he wrote a letter to the Trotters, informing them that he was now a Royal guard and serving the Princess, whom he saved her back then and asked how everyone else were, after he was gone.

Next morning was his first Sunday of his duty. He went with the Princess and the King along with Harrison in one carriage and with some other guards, who were on horses riding along with them, to the church. After the mass, Alister ordered to stop near an Earl's house named Lord Anton. They went inside and Daniel found Oliver, one of the four guards who were with him. He worked as one of the guards of Anton. They gave a pale smile to each other with a nod and stood by their master's side. Their masters excuse from them for privacy and they went out along with Evelyn and Harrison.

"Daniel, watch the King and the Princess, I'm going to check the carriage", said Harrison.

Daniel nodded once as yes. Harrison went out and he watched the Princess. She started to run in the hallway.

"Princess, be careful. Don't run out of my site", he insisted.

"Don't worry, no one is going to hurt her", interrupted Oliver.

"How can you be sure?"

"I work here, brother."

"I'm not going too far", she replied.

"So, Harrison gave you to guard the Princess", said Oliver.

"So, what's the odd about it?"

Oliver sighed. "Have you heard about Eric...?" Suddenly Alister and Anton came out.

"It is him", said Alister, addressing to Daniel and they stood in attention. "He saved Evelyn, ten months ago."

"So, you are Daniel Ewart?" asked Anton.

"Yes, my Lord", he replied.

Anton looked at him and then he turned to the King. "See you later, My Lord", he said.

"All right, My Lord", replied Alister.

They excused and started returning to the palace. One the way they stopped. Two carts had collapsed on the road and the owners were quarrelling and blaming the mistake on each other and people had gathered around. Harrison came out and burst on them that they both were blocking the King's way and he ordered two of his men to arrest them. Daniel also came out and saw Harrison scolding the two people but the carts were still on the road. He saw some man watching the scenario and asked them to come and help him out. They came and they lifted the carts with Daniel and moved them aside.

Unexpectedly, Daniel caught the sight of a woman watching him. She walked away when he looked at her. Harrison warned the two cart owners and let them go, this time. They sat back into the carriage and returned to the palace. The day of duty was over and he returned back to his chamber and thought about the day events by lying on his bed. He thought about meeting Oliver and what he was speaking about a person, which he forgot. Then he remembered about the women at the market place and kept on thinking about him and felt like he had seen her somewhere.

Next day his duty went as usual. Then on the second day, when his duty was over, he was returning back to his chamber and he accidently bumped onto a maid, carrying clothes and it fell on the ground.

"Forgive me, it was my mistake", he said and tried to help her.

"Please don't", she said. "I can do it by myself", and didn't even looked to him.

Daniel moved back. She picked the clothes and went on her way. He returned to his chamber, lies on his bed and wondered who she was? She seemed pretty and familiar. And then he remembered her face. She was the women at the market, no wonder why he felt that he had seemed her before. She works in the palace and a couple of times, he had seen her but not directly. Next morning when he went to the staff dining room, he saw her again, serving the chef and others. He thought, she will be serving him too but she didn't and went away and another newly young maid named Eva served him. In the coming days, he got the same response from her but not by others. Thought another worker he learnt that her name was Agnes Dunber and she was working for four years.

After ten days of writing a letter, he received a reply letter from the Trotters. They told them that after he left, Lewis and Larry had to do his part of work. The work became more for them but later it became usual. Then they also congratulated him and hoped he was doing great at his duty. They also told him that Lewis introduced his lover, Rachael to the family. She was a shy girl and doesn't talk much and they were thinking about the wedding and her father had agreed too. She was the only daughter of her father and her father wanted Lewis to own his farmland after him and he was learning how to harvest and everything was moving great.

Daniel sighed, never thought that things will be changed after he will be gone. He remembered the first day when he was first introduced with Trotters and now he was here. All of a sudden he remembered about Agnes Dunber, he thought she must also be shy and that's why she doesn't want to be near him. So next day, he paid a servant to buy some flowers for him and he bought it from the market and he delivered it to him after his duty. Then he asked Eva to deliver the flowers to Agnes, with a note explaining to her that she doesn't need to be shy, she was free to ask him. And Eva did it, without asking why?

Next morning, before having the breakfast at the staff dining room, Hilda an old maid stopped Daniel and talked with him.

"What is the matter?" asked Daniel.

"Daniel, did you send flowers to Agnes thought Eva?" she asked.

"Yes, I did, well she was a shy woman, so I told her that she should be free to talk with me."

"It is completely opposite that what you are thinking about her... when Eva gave that flowers to her and told that it was from you, she became angry and scolded her."

"What? Why? I don't get it?" he was astonished.

"Listen Daniel, please don't get harsh, I have settled that matter among them..."

"But why is she so angry?"

Hilda looked around; no one was close to them. "Well, do you know a person named Eric Dunber?"

"Ahh... No I don't."

Hilda explained that Eric Dunber was the guard of the Princess before him and he was the older brother of Agnes and he was executed to fail at his duty and leaving the Princess into the forest while returning from a place. Before execution, he was given the order to find the Princess because her protection was his responsibility but he failed and Daniel found her instead for which Agnes blamed him. After hearing that Daniel was shocked because he had no idea of Eric. He blamed Harrison for not telling him about Eric. He went to met him but he wasn't in the palace. A foot guard told him that he was out with the King early in the morning. Daniel waited and Harrison returned with the King in the evening.

He waited for a moment. Then the King walked his way to his room while Harrison approached to the direction where Daniel was standing. Later something occurred in Daniel's mind and he decided not to take the matter any further. Harrison found Daniel standing.

"Whom are you waiting for?" he asked.

"No one, I was just about to go", he replied and went.

As he was going to the Princess chamber he met Eva. She was sobbing. The reason was Agnes. She scolded her again.

"Okay I would talk to her", decided Daniel, pissed.

He wanted to meet Agnes immediately but then he remembered his duty and stood outside the room of the Princess.

After the duty, he found Agnes with three maids in the washing chamber. She noticed him but she didn't pay any attention to him and kept on working and talking to her fellow maids. But Daniel came close to her and said, "Miss Dunber I'm here to talk. I want to apologise about your brother. You can blame me if you want but why did you scold Eva, again. She did no wrong. She only did what I requested her."

"Mr. Ewart, I'm sorry that I scolded her", said Agnes, harshly, "but what because of you had happened is unforgivable...." the three maids walked behind. "Do you know what family is? You don't know anything. My brother was my only family left to me after our parents died and because of you, he was taken away from me."

Daniel could have said that Eric was careless and the Princess went missing but he kept his mind calm.

He laughed once, "You say I don't know about family... I think you are right. I could have been a better person if I had my mother and my father since birth. But when I found a family who cared about me, I left them so that they could have their own life and I have my own but I guess it was another mistake. I have done mistake but nobody told me what and I kept on doing that mistake, over and over but thanks to you. You were the first person who told me my mistake and I won't repeat it again?"

"I'm not interested in your rubbish story", she interrupted.

The other three maids got scared because Agnes was arguing with a Royal guard which could let her to serious punishments.

"Okay then my deepest apologies for my misunderstanding", he said. "But if you say anything to Eva, I will defend her. Consider this as my mercy", and walked out of the room.

After few moments, Agnes cooled down and felt really bad on her rude attitude to him but she was still angry. At some point, she believed that it was his brother's fault that got him killed but then she thought, if Daniel wouldn't have interrupted, the Princess could be saved by Eric and he would be still alive. She was trying to hate Daniel as much as possible for the cause of her brother's execution which was very difficult for her now because he had taken his place.

Like this, she couldn't concentrate on her work and then one day she accidently dropped the silver dishes on the way to the washing chamber. Daniel was approaching from the opposite direction and saw her accident. She noticed him standing but she ignored him. Daniel too didn't pay any attention and walked passing by her but at the same time, Harrison and the chief chef reached, chatting about food and saw the accident.

"What the heck happened?" asked Harrison.

"Are those Royal dishes?" asked the chef, noticing it.

She got scared and kept on picking.

"Agnes! Are those Royal dishes", the chef asked, angrily. "Where is your mind?"

"Pardon me please", she replied.

"How can you make such mistake?" he moved close looking down to her, but at the same moment, Daniel came on his way.

"Wait, hold on right there", said Daniel and the chef turned to him.

"It was my fault, I was walking and I got bumped into her", he claimed.

The chef looked into his eyes and was angry that he was interrupted.

"Pardon me, people, let us pretend that nothing had happened here... right", interrupted Harrison, politely.

Then the chef walked on his way with Harrison. Daniel helped her picking up the dishes and then they went on their respected works. Later in the evening Eva informed Daniel that Agnes wanted to talk with him. Daniel was little amazed that why she want to meet her? Anyway, he went after his duty was over. She was waiting near the door of the hallway to servant's chambers.

"You want to talk with me?" he asked her.

"Yes", she answered.

"So what is about?"

"I just, I just want to apologise about what I said that night."

"What changed your mind?" he asked.

"Just I don't know why but... And I have also apologised to Eva too."

Daniel sighed and nodded and turned to walk away.

"Mr. Ewart wait..." she stopped him.

"What?" he asked her.

"Why you saved me this noon? You could have left me."

"Then what, you could have been expelled and where would you have gone then."

"Are you trying to be nice?"

"No, just following someone's footsteps who gave me a pair of different boot which didn't fit well", he answered. "He told me- Always be good to yourself no matter how cruel response you get from the world, least you won't feel guilty when your breath end."

And then he walked away. Those were the last words said by Wilson to Daniel when he was taking his last breath. The following day, he was with the Princess in the garden. She was having a tea with her friend, daughter of an Earl, Lord Grant. He was talking with Alister joyfully on the other side of the garden. Suddenly, Daniel turned and saw Agnes walking by holding the laundry, staring at him. She quickly turned straight and left Daniel surprised.

One day Daniel went with Evelyn to meet her grandmother Olivia and while returning it was very late and Daniel hadn't eaten anything. He was given to eat which he refused because it was getting dark for them to return. When they returned, he immediately went into the Royal kitchen to get himself to eat but he couldn't found it. There were vegetable and flours but all of them were raw. Then he heard step noise and turned and saw a maid with washed dishes.

"Excuse me, is there something left for me to eat?" he asked. The maid was Agnes. "Oh... sorry, I guess there is nothing left", he said and turned to go.

"Wait there is some soup and a loaf is left... if you want I can make the soup warm", said Agnes, when he was near the door.

He felt awkward. "Okay..." he replied.

He waited at the table and then she served him with a bowl of hot soup and a loaf. He started to eat and she went to arrange the plates which she just washed.

"What were you doing so late?" he asked her, chewing.

"Washing and keeping staffs dishes."

"Do you work like this all the night?"

"No, not always", she replied. "We wash by taking turns and today Eva was sick today, so I came in her place", and kept the final plate on the shelf and turned to him. "And why are you so late?"

"Got late at grandmother's house, Princess's grandmothers", he answered.

"I see", she said then she removed her hair cover and let her blonde hair was free.

Releasing her hairs, she looked prettier to him. He felt hard to move his eyes away from her.

"Mr. Ewart I want to apologies", she said.

"Apologies for what? And please call me Daniel."

"Do you know when that night I told you... recklessly about family that... you don't know and all that...? I didn't know that, I really regret it very much."

"No, no, please Miss Dunber, you don't have to. It's fine. You only don't know much about me. And I Apologies too, for sending those... flowers, I should have asked someone else about you, first."

"That's okay and I tossed the flowers into the garbage. And please call me Agnes", she requested and sat on the bench opposite to him.

They paused for a moment.

"Good night Mr. Ewart", she said and he watched her till she was out of the door.

One evening, Daniel received a wedding invitation letter. It was from Mr. Trotter, noticing him that after two weeks Lewis was getting married to Rachael.

Congratulation, you finally found your girl, he greeted him in his though. He planned for the gifts and the dress he should wear on that day and he waited. He then saw Agnes working and thought of taking her too. He asked her and she said that she will think about it and she thought and it took two days to decide but finally she said yes. But there was still a problem and that was Harrison. He won't allow two Royal servants to take a day off. He thought of giving a gift, clothes or something precious, but all of them were a nonsense idea to convince him.

One noon, three days before the wedding, he was in the library wondering how to convince the Commander.

"Daniel, Daniel, can you get me that book" called Evelyn, pulling his shirt.

He noticed, "Oh sorry Princess, what were you saying?"

"Can you get that book from that shelf? Then he raises his hand and brought it down.

"Where you been so lost?" she asked him.

"My apologies Princess… it was just I cannot decide."

"Decide what?"

"Well… one of my brothers, I mean, he is like my brother is getting married and I'm invited…"

"Then take that day off and have a visit", suggested Evelyn, simply.

"I have decided to visit there but there is some other personal matter."

"What is the other personal matter?" Daniel paused, he doesn't want to say it but neither he what to tell a lie the Princess but then he realized something.

"Princess", he said.

"What is it?"

"Can you do me a favour? Just for one time." he insisted.

She turned to him and paused.

"Maybe", she replied.

Daniel told her about his matter that he wants to take Agnes to the wedding day and instead she had to convince Harrison so that he could give her a day off too. Evelyn agreed and she personally asked permission and Harrison got no other choice but to give Agnes and Daniel a day off.

"Very clever move, Ewart, very clever move", said Harrison, in his thought.

The wedding day arrived. Daniel dressed great and waited for Agnes outside the palace. She arrived wearing a cloak. She doesn't know how to ride a horse so they sat on one horse and rode gently fast towards the village church. They arrived just in time and so do the other guests. Actually they were the last guests to arrive and the church was not even that crowd hardly eight families with least four members had gathered and most of them were from the bride's side. Agnes removed her cloak and exposed her beautiful dress. She was wearing it inside the cloak so that the palace guard won't flirt with her.

"Nice dress", said Daniel.

"Thank you", she replied, with a smile.

"Hey son, over here", said Mr. Trotter and gave him a warm hug and so do Mrs. Trotter and Larry and they also warmly hugged Agnes, smiling.

Daniel waved hand to Lewis and he waved back with a smile and Rachael was dressed beautifully like an angel from heaven and was little nervous and so do Lewis. Daniel and Agnes were given the seat and then the priest started the mass and then the couple said the vow and finally, kissing the bride and the people applauded.

The reception was done at the inn and then three musicians, who were hired, started playing their bagpipes instruments and the family members and the new couple started dancing. Daniel was pulled to join the dance and later Agnes. All of them enjoyed the moment, until the day turned evening and then the party ended and everybody congratulated the new couple and returned home.

Daniel was preparing his horse ready when Lewis arrived.

"Hey brother", he said and they hugged.

"Congratulation", greeted Daniel, joyfully.

"Thank you, Thank you... Hey what with you and Agnes", asked Lewis.

Daniel looked to her; she was talking to Rachael and Mrs. Trotter.

"No, we aren't", he answered.

"No?"

"No, we are just friends. I just messed up something and so I brought her to make up mind", he replied, simply.

Then all the family members arrived and hugged Daniel and Agnes goodbye. Agnes wore her cloak and they sat on the horse and returned. She was very happy and kept on smiling all the way back. It was her best moment in her entire life which she would never forget. Then they said good night to each other and parted their way to their chambers, smiling. Agnes returned to her chamber, changed her dress and laid on her bed facing to the roof. There were three more maids sleeping in the same chamber. She was still smiling and thinking about the day fun when she saw a locket, hanging on the wall, near her bed. She rose up and took it on her hand and laid back. It was a gift from his brother.

Daniel too returned to his chamber but he wasn't tired. He wore his guard uniform and went to check the Princess. As he was passing through the hallway, he heard someone talking. He was going to ignore it but as the talking mentioned the killing of Eric Dunber, it made him stop. He thought he must have misheard, but he followed the voice.

"Give me more money or I'll expose your bloody sin."

"Two days ago I had paid you."

"But I want more."

"You are such a greedy person."

He came to a turn of the hallway and at a few distances and saw Harrison and the chief chef were arguing.

"Of course I'm but I'm not the murderer", replied the chef.

"No one will believe you, it is been over one year", said Harrison.

"No, that you think. And you are not in the position to rule of over, I rule over you until you die."

"What if you die first?"

The chef sighed. "Harrison let me remind you about Eric Dunber for the last time that you are the reason that he was executed."

"How are you going to prove that I convicted falsely and he was executed?"

Daniel was shocked when he heard that.

"I will just go and tell the King that you did and with little sobbing drama, he will consider and I'll win... and I also know that you have told a different tale to the Princess, right", said the chef, smiling at him.

Harrison got pissed and caught his sword's handle. "Be careful to what you speak", he warned but the chef was not threatened.

"Before you kill me, remember that there are three chefs, who are like my best friends, and they also obey me and respect me a lot. Whenever I go to met you, I always tell them that I was going to meet you and also thought me, the King know their names well. So if you kill me... then think about it and don't forget by tomorrow", said the chef, turned and walked away.

Harrison was filled with rage; he took a deep breath and cooled himself. Suddenly he heard breathing noise from behind. He turned and walked to that turn and found no one was there. He was frustrated and angry but somehow, he cooled himself. He went to the Princess's room to check her.

"Is Princess, still inside?" he asked the door guard.

"Yes sir and Daniel too."

"Daniel?" he was surprised. "When did he come?"

"A few moments ago..."

He walked inside and found them arranging books from the shelf.

"Daniel, when did you arrive?" he asked.

"Just a while ago", he replied.

"I thought you had a day off."

"I was not tired so, I came to check the Princess."

Harrison sighed and said good night to the Princess and walked out the room. He went into his chamber and drank some wine. After few minutes, Daniel also returned to his chamber. He thought about the talk between Harrison and the chief chef. He assumed that Eric Dunber execution was some kind of conspiracy and Harrison was the mastermind and the chef was blackmailing for money. He tried to ignore it because he doesn't want to get involved in that matter but he couldn't. He hated himself that why he decided to go and check the Princess in the first place. If he had stayed in his chamber then he wouldn't have heard them talking and his peace of mind won't be disturbed.

He rose up and pressed his head, it was very hard for him to forget. He looked to the walls and the door, thinking what to do? How to forget about it? Then he realized that he was sleeping in the chamber, where once Eric Dunber slept. He felt and heard the cry as if Eric was crying for help and then he remembered about Agnes, she once also hate him that he was responsible for her brother's death and maybe still hating.

After a lot of thinking, Daniel decided that he will get close to that fact or else he would be next or maybe some other innocent or it could be the Princess herself. He looked to his uniform and remembered that he was the Royal guard and it was his duty to guard not only the Princess but also the innocent people in the palace. He thought who to ask about Eric Dunber would be better? Because now no one seemed to be trusted and suspected that Harrison knew that he had heard their conversation and if he asked someone and he might tell it to Harrison, he could be in big trouble. While thinking he remembered about Oliver, telling him about a person named Eric. He didn't mention his last name but he thought he must be talking about him.

When the Sunday arrived, he got the chance to meet Oliver. He was also with his master at the church and when the King Alister, Anton and the Cardinal were talking. He asked Oliver about the person he was talking about that day and he couldn't remember telling him about any person.

"Okay then, tell me what you know about Eric Dunber? He was a Royal guard before me. Do you remember anything?" he asked.

"Never heard of..." he answered and then their respective masters called them and they went on their duties.

All the way coming back to the palace, Daniel thought what to do? Whom to ask? One person was Oliver and now he had forgotten. Harrison was sitting right in front of him, in the carriage along with the King and the Princess and if he tells the King directly, he will be the one in trouble. Then he thought about talking to the Princess, it was risky but he got no other choice and he also feared that she might have forgotten.

Before getting back to his duty, he met Hilda and he asked her about Eric Dunber. He remembered mentioning about Eric Dunber about leavening the Princess, getting into the forest while returning from the place.

"Can you tell me about Eric Dunber?" he asked.

"Why all of a sudden you want to know?"

"I'm just curious to know that what mistake he made that he was executed and I don't want to repeat that."

She thought hard and answered that one day the King and her daughter had gone to a party and while returning Eric and the Princess left the party early and were returning on their respective horses. Suddenly something frightened the horse and the horse went crazy and it ran into the forest, taking the Princess with her. Instead of going after him Eric returned to the palace. The King and Harrison were very angry and they send him back to get her which he failed and then executed on the next day.

After her statement, he felt like Eric indeed was responsible for his own execution but still he didn't understand how Harrison was involved. That same noon when he was in the garden with the Princess and no one was around, he gained himself some courage and asked, "Princess, do- do you remember that night when we first met and I helped you."

She looked to him and said, "When we first met? What are you talking about?"

His fear about she might have forgotten came true but he continued, "That night when you were lost in the forest and you came to my door and asked for help and I help you and then next morning I carried you on my back and took you half way till the palace."

"I don't remember any of... oh, now I remember, yes, I remember..." she claimed.

Daniel felt relief. "Can you tell me exactly how you got lost that day...? I just remembered and I was just curious about it", he asked.

"Well I was riding a horse and it went crazy... and I fell and I don't know where I wandered and then I found your house", she answered.

"So, did Eric Dunber the guard before me, did something that your horse went crazy?"

"Eric Dunber?"

"He was travelling with you that day, isn't he?"

"No, he wasn't. It was Harrison, who was travelling with me that day and as far as I remember, Eric went early to get something from the palace", she answered. "I thought he was a nice person. But he tried to steal gold from the Royal treasure and he was caught by Harrison and executed, which every criminal should get."

Daniel was shocked but he was also confused that why Hilda told him a different story?

"Pardon me Princess, but I heard he was executed for leading you into the forest."

"I have already told you everything I know. Why don't you ask Harrison about it?"

"Harrison?"

"Yes Harrison, he told me that why Dunber was executed?"

"Does your father know about this?"

"Of Course he does, Harrison was the one who caught him."

After the duty, back in his chamber, he thought why Hilda told him a different story? Then he thought to ask Agnes about it but he felt it wasn't the right time to talk to her. Next morning Lord Anton came to meet the King and in that way, he met Oliver again and he told him that he remembered about Eric Dunber by asking another guard of the house where he works.

"Okay tell me why he was executed?" asked Daniel.

"I learnt that when he was returning with the Princess, the horse on which the Princess was riding went crazy and took her into the forest and instead of going after her, he came to the palace and the King was very angry and he sent him back which he failed."

"How many of you know this story... I mean this incidence?"

"All the guards at Lord Anton's house and they told me about this."

"Oh."

"But why are you asking this, I thought you would have known by now."

"Yes, I know. I was just..."

"Is everything okay?"

Then Oliver was called by one of his college guards and he said, "Okay I'm going now. Take care of yourself", and went on his duty.

In the noon, during the lunch time, he asked a guard named Holmes about Eric Dunber and he gave a similar answer like Oliver and Hilda and another guard who was with him also agreed and they also told that it was told by Harrison. Now he understood that why the statement of Princess was not similar to the statement of the people whom he asked? It was confirmed that Princess Evelyn was actually telling him the truth about what had happened with her and other were telling, what they had been told by Harrison.

But still he had a blank which was to be filled and that was where Eric Dunber was at that time when Harrison and Evelyn were returning and why he didn't appealed? He could have saved himself. He thought to ask Hilda again but then he felt that it was not a good idea or she might suspect something was going wrong. After thinking a lot, he thought to ask Agnes about it. Later after the duty, he called her to his chamber and told her everything that that day when they arrived from Lewis's wedding, he accidently heard Harrison and the chief chef were talking about his brother and what Hilda and some other guards including Oliver told him and what Princess told him. He considered that Eric wasn't even with Evelyn when she went missing. It was Harrison. Hearing that, she was shocked and couldn't bear to stand.

"What are you talking about? My brother framed by Harrison? How even that possible?" she said.

"See, during the trial, was he convicted that he had stolen, Royal treasure?" She didn't reply. She was still in shock. "Agnes!" then he responded and he asked her again.

She thought and replied, "No, no he wasn't convicted that..."

"Then was he convicted for leaving the Princess?"

She didn't reply. He went close to her and caught her shoulders and said, "Hey don't be silent."

"I can't..." she replied and started to cry. "I don't know what to do? What to tell?"

"Hey, hey look at, look at me", she looked at him and he turned her around and said, "look, this was your brother's chamber, isn't it? He could have been resting here now after his duty if he was alive... When I first heard the conversation, I wanted to ignore it but I couldn't because I felt someone else will die, sooner or later and I won't let that happened", he walked in front of her. "Help me, speak out, let me help your brother and let's punish those bastards who frame your brother."

Agnes got some encouragement and she answered that during the trial he wasn't convicted of stealing the Royal property but was convicted for leaving the Princess into the forest.

"Okay then, tell me, what was your brother doing that day, when the Royals had gone for the party at Lord Caster?"

She answered that his brother was also gone in the party and nothing else but then she remembered that he returned early and she remembered when he passed by her. He said that he was there to take some contract papers for Lord Caster from Harrison's office and he returned and then he returned alone. The far she remembers that he was sent out again by the King and Harrison which she learnt from a foot guard.

It was now considered that they went to the party and Eric must have been sent by Harrison to collect the papers and he came and went back. During that time period, Harrison and Princess were returning and then the incident happened and when Eric returned back after giving those papers to Lord Caster, he was held responsible for that. He didn't speak because he had his oath and agreed his mistake and went to search but he didn't found her.

Then Agnes told him that she want to punish the Commander at all cost, even it would take to poison his drink. Daniel recommended not taking such reckless action against a person who was famous and pious. He was a wolf under a sheep's skin but there was a way to expose him. The way was Evelyn. Agnes felt relieved that there was hope and it won't fail to get justice for his brother.

Daniel hugged her when suddenly a maid cried out. The Royal staff's sleep was broken and they ran to find out, who screamed? And when they arrived at the Royal kitchen from where the maid screamed, they all were shocked; the chief chef was bleeding dead on the ground covered with flour. He was murdered. Daniel and Agnes arrived at the spot and were also shocked and more was Daniel. The palace night guards arrived and asked them to move aside and were also stunned. One of the guards named Norval said to another, "Call Commander Harrison and get the King to safety, the wounds seemed fresh, close the palace gates might the killer be still hiding inside the palace go!"

Daniel kept gazing him. He was bleeding from the chest. He got a feeling that he knew who did this?

"Hey, Daniel, Daniel", called Norval.

"Yes."

"Go to the Princess chamber and be with her night guards."

"Okay", he replied, nodding and went.

Agnes followed him out. "Daniel, wait..." she said, terrified. "The chef, murdered?" she said.

He went close to her. "I think I know who did this?" he whispered.

"Who?"

"It's Harrison."

"What are you going to do? How will you prove him guilty?"

"Don't forget I told you about the Princess, she is a key to show him guilty, I'm going to watch her and you should go and be with someone, don't stay alone. I think he knows what we have known", and he ran.

As he was few distance away from Evelyn's chamber, he encountered Harrison.

"Daniel... what are you doing here? And who screamed?" said Harrison making an astonishing face.

Daniel got terrified by his sudden encounter but he made himself to look calm.

"There's been a murder", replied Daniel, "The chief chef is murdered and I'm here to guard Evelyn but what are you doing here? You should be going at the murder spot."

"I'm here to guard the Princess..." he replied and at the same time, Daniel saw some stained flour on Harrison's pants and shoes. Then he remembered there was flour scattered around the ground where the chef was murdered. Harrison caught his view and looked down to see what he was gazing at and he saw his pants stained with white flour.

"Oh God", said Harrison, he had understood that Daniel had discovered his sins.

"I think you got me, Mr. Ewart", declared Harrison. "I'm curious, how much you know about me?"

"Tell me why you framed Eric? Is it because you will lose your job?"

Harrison laughed. "Lose my job? Mr. Ewart let me tell you something which you don't know. There is one thing that man losses in one strike, which takes him decades to build. That is dignity."

"You killed a kind man, just for your dignity and threatened his sister to kill and now the second, the chef."

"I think, I misjudge you, Mr. Ewart. I should have caught your cleverness when you used the Princess's power to take a day off with that bastard maid."

"Her name is Agnes. She was the sister of Eric and you took her away from her."

"Damn you, Ewart."

"Tell me you did kill the chef for blackmailing?"

Harrison sighed and then replied, "I was about to kill him when we were having the conversation that day."

"So you knew, I was there and listening to your conversation that night."

"Obviously and beside the chef also told me you were talking a lot with the Princess about Eric. Poor chef, I love his cooking and loved a lot more than my mother's. And have you ever wondered why I choose you to be the Princess guard."

"No, it doesn't matter", said Daniel.

"The answer is... you were a pawn, Ewart. You were a pawn. When the chef found out about framing Eric, he was going to tell the King but I stopped him and paid him some handsome amount but then, later on, he started blackmailed me and I have to vanish him as soon as possible but the problem was he was the chef and he cooks food for all the people under the palace and I could be suspected easily, if I would have taken action against him and I didn't want to be suspected. Then I remembered about you. You were perfect whom I could blame the murder and so here we are just as planned and I have waited over a year and it's worth it."

"None of this matter Commander or should I call just call you a murderer", declared Daniel, "there is no escape for you, I'm going to arrest you and bring Eric and the chef to King's justice", drawing his sword.

"You are going to arrest me, sorry Ewart; I'm here to kill you. I have placed the blood knife in your chamber and everyone will suspect you that you had killed the chef", said Harrison.

For a moment Daniel thought he was doomed but then he replied, "I have a witness and her name is Agnes."

"Oh thanks, for telling her name". Then he realized that he shouldn't have told her name.

"But still you will be locked in jail."

"You are indeed a clever person, Ewart but... the one think you lack is power, you don't have the power to put me in my own dungeons. The King is my best friend since childhood and I'll convince him anyway."

"You may have the King but... I have the Princess. She was there when you sent Eric and she will not hesitate to act as a witness."

Harrison laughed, "Oh really, how could she remember the event that happened a year ago?"

"Of course, she does and I made her to remember. You cannot kill her either to save your bloody dignity. And how did you forget that the chef told you that I was talking to her?"

Harrison got pissed and draws up his sword and attacked Daniel. They had the duel. During swinging Daniel's blade struck Harrison's chain and the gold cross fell on the ground but still, they kept on fighting until Daniel's sword fell from his hand. Harrison pushed him to the wall on his sword point and said, "Daniel, Daniel, you are a very clever person like I said but I'm more clever, good sword fighter and more powerful than you. You are not the Daniel whom God saved him from hungry lions. Now die."

Daniel closed his eyes and unexpectedly somebody stabbed Harrison from behind with Daniel's sword and pulled it out of his flesh and he failed to stab Daniel. He turned and found that it was Agnes.

"That is for my brother", she declared, angrily and also scared.

He grunted and fell on the ground. Daniel took the sword from her hand then they ran to the Princess chamber but they didn't find her. The King arrived with four of his guards and found Harrison dying.

"Who did this? Tell me his name", asked the King, shocked and angry.

Harrison spoke the name of Daniel and Agnes into Alister's ear and died. Evelyn could have saved them but now they were in trouble as they heard their names calling by the guard to be captured. Daniel decided to get out from the palace or the guards would kill them. They managed to get into guards dressing room and they disguised themselves like foot guards and covered their faces with the helmet. They came out from the palace from a side palace door and walked to the stable. They took two horses by pulling its bridle and walked to the gate.

"Where you both are going?" asked the gate guard.

"The King has commanded us to look outside for the fugitives", replied Daniel, feared to be caught. The guard doubted but then Daniel spoke in a loud voice, "Are you listening to me there was a murder inside the palace and why are you working like a slug." The gate guard got no other choice but to let them out.

"Princess Evelyn is safe", said one guard to the King.

Alister felt relieved and then he came out of the palace and asked the gate guard.

"Did somebody tried to run out from the gate?" asked Alister.

"No Your Majesty, except for our two guards that you ordered to patrol outside", replied the gate guard.

Alister was amazed.

"What? But I haven't ordered anyone to go out", claimed the King.

They were two of them and they suspected it could be them, who murdered the chef and Harrison. The King with eight of his men quickly rode on their respective horses and chased them, holding torches and armed with swords.

They found one horse on the street of city Zeus and it was their palace horse. They concluded that they are going in the right direction and rode as fast as they could. They kept riding and came out of the city and few distances away they saw a horse by two people. It was a full moon night and the armour which Daniel and Agnes were wearing shinned slightly by the moonlight and they considered it will be them and were right. Agnes heard some galloping noises and she looked back. It was King Alister and his men.

Daniel gave a shock to the horse's rein and the horse started to run even faster. Then he turned his horse into the forest to get rid of them. The King's horse stopped and reared. The forest was dark and scary and the moonlight didn't even reach the surface.

"Where we going?" asked Agnes.

"A safe place", he answered and stall the horse. "We should walk, or else they will catch the foot of the horse."

They climbed down from the horse and he kicked on horses back and the horse ran away. They kept on walking until they arrived at a hut which was Daniel's home and they tossed the armours outside the house. He hadn't locked it as there was nothing to be stolen. They got inside and took a little rest by sitting on the bed.

"Whose house is this?" she asked.

"Mine, actually a person named Wilson."

"What happened to him?"

"He died in sleep."

They remained silent for a moment and Daniel thought about his next move which he couldn't think of. He looked at the door and remembered the knock of that day and how it all started.

"Daniel, I think we can do nothing, now", said Agnes and caught her shivering hands.

"Hey don't worry, there is always a way", he replied, holding her hand.

"No, Daniel not this time. I have killed a person and he was not an ordinary person and I will be executed, no matter what and you will be too..."

"Don't say that..."

"Listen Daniel, you have taken a lot of trouble and thank you for that and now it's my turn to return the favour."

"What favour?"

"Daniel, I'll surrender myself to them. You will have enough time to live this country."

"No, no don't speak like that", he protested.

"Then what shall we do?"

"We will both get out of this country."

Suddenly they heard galloping sounds, outside. It was the King and his guards. They somehow tracked them.

"We know you are in there, Ewart and that maid Dunber!" said Norvel. "Surrender yourself or we will burn your little house!"

Agnes got terrified, she caught Daniel's arm.

"We haven't murdered the chef. It was Commander Harrison. He murdered him!" cried Daniel. Everybody felt awkward, and then Norval replied, "But Commander Harrison is dead and he told our Majesty that you killed him and that makes possible that you too killed the chef."

"I don't have any reason to kill anyone. Go check Commander Harrison's pants and you will find some flour, must have stained when he killed the chef." They looked to each other and Alister gave him the signal to continue talking.

"If there is some flour, we can assume that you must have put some on him to frame him?"

"I didn't frame him. Commander Harrison framed Eric and killed the chef. Killing Harrison was self-defence", claimed Daniel.

"Do you have any witness?" Daniel paused and looked to Agnes.

"Yes, I'm the witness!" cried Agnes. "I'm Agnes Dunber and my brother Eric Dunber was the Royal guard of the Princess which Harrison farmed and he was executed for a false crime which he didn't commit and I killed Commander Harrison, in order to protect Daniel. It was self-defence, Your Majesty."

"Then why did you ran away!" interrupted Alister. "Only a criminal runs away in fear of getting caught." No reply came. "Surrender yourself or we will burn you alive in there."

"But we did not kill him", cried Daniel. "We ran because we have the fear to get killed."

"Fear?" repeated Alister, "that is what I was talking about? You feared that you will be killed because you killed them. You murderers!"

They got no chance to run; they were right in front of their door. Alister was very angry and he said that why they were talking to a couple of criminals and he ordered his men to burn them inside. The guard's hesitated a little but the King forced them to do and they set fire on the hut. The house started to burn. They heard their cry as the fire rampaged the house. They waited if they come out by chance, they could kill them. Then as the fire took all over the house there was no crying and the fire turned everything to dust. Life of Daniel ended where he got the second chance to start along with Agnes. Alister and his men returned back to the palace.

Next day the guards returned back to the same spot and collected some scraps including the Royal sword of Daniel whose charming blade colour had become dark by fire and smoke. Then on the second day after the night incident, three of King's soldiers arrived at Trotter's Inn and told them about Daniel's death. Mrs. Trotter couldn't handle the burden and started to sob. Lewis and Larry went to see the resident of Daniel but there was nothing left to see, only ashes.

Then something happened, rumours about Daniel and Agnes started to spread all over the kingdom like a rapid fire that they were innocent and the King killed them without giving them a trial. The citizens of Zeus protested near the palace gate and even the Royal servants demanded a proper answer that they were criminals. And so a Royal council meeting was organized to verify the matter.

Lord Mungo, Lord Grant, Lord Caster and Lord Anton including the King's mother Olivia and Cardinal Errol assembled at the throne chamber for the judiciary. Three guards who trained with Daniel were also present too. They were been given in charge, one for the Cardinal, Lord Mungo and Lord Caster. Other people including Mr. Trotter and Larry were also present in the chamber to hear the judgment including all the Royal staff.

"Since the King is a witness of the incident, I'll be the judge of the trial and Lord Caster will question", declared the Cardinal. "So we have gathered here to know whether Daniel and Agnes are innocent or criminals... Present the evidence."

Two guards came holding a knife which was stained with blood, which was dry and placed it on the table. They both took the oath that they will speak the truth and one of them said, "My Lord, this is the knife which was used to kill the head chef of this palace."

"How can you both be so sure?" Asked Lord Caster.

"My Lord, when Your Majesty ordered to arrest Daniel the former Royal guard and a maid... and sorry I forgot her name... I along with him went to his chamber to arrest him but he was not there but we found this knife beside the doorsteps, seemed like it fell while he was trying to run out of the chamber."

"Yes that is what happened that night and I was there", said the other.

"And what about Harrison, did he got killed by that knife?" asked Caster.

"No not with this..."

Alister interrupted and explained that Harrison was killed by a sword because when he arrived with four guards, he was bleeding from back and chest. The sword had gone through him and when asked who did this to him, he whispered their names into his ears, Daniel Ewart and Agnes Dunber.

The sword was shown which had come black by the fire but the King's statement and the four guards witness were enough for it. Thus it was considered that Daniel had killed them and Agnes had supported him. Mungo, Anton and Grant looked to each other and nodded that the evidence shows that they were indeed the murderers. The people present also nodded and agreed except for the Trotters.

"So is there anyone who wants to speak anything for them?" asked Caster.

Larry stood up. "My Lord, I want to speak something."

"And you?"

"My name is Larry Trotter and Daniel Ewart was like my brother to me. He was a like a family and as far as I know him, he wouldn't murder someone like this. He will never do such thing", he answered.

"We have the evidence and the witnesses. Do you have something then present it now and stop wasting time", said Anton.

"Y-yes My Lord, I have something", he answered and that left everyone curious.

"And what exactly do you have?" asked Caster.

Larry took out a letter and said, "Daniel was in contact with us, thought writing letters and this one was his last one. It has everything that is needed."

Caster took the letter and read it. It had explained that the night when they came back from Lewis's wedding he heard Harrison and the chef talking about money in which the chief chef warned Harrison that if he doesn't pay him more money, he will expose that he was the one responsible when the Princess went lost and he blamed all the charges on her Royal guard named Eric Dunber and he was executed. And if he tried to kill him, he had three chefs, whom he always tell them that he was going to meet Harrison and anything happened to him, blame Harrison and they also serve the King and the Princess during meal time. As the honour of being the Royal guards, he decided to investigate and asked Hilda and Oliver who was the guard of Lord Anton and they replied that Eric Dunber left the Princess in the woods but that was not true. They were only telling that because that what they heard during the trial but when he asked the Princess, she said that she was returning with Harrison, not Eric and she told that Eric was executed because he was trying to steal Royal treasure which was also told by Harrison and he felt that he was going to die. And in the end, he had signed his full name.

Everyone was shocked after hearing the letter. Mungo, Anton, Grant, Olivia and Alister protested that it was nonsense that Larry had made up the letter but Larry said that his father was his witness that they had received the letter and they don't know any people who were mentioned in the letters. They were also present in the chamber. First, they want to confirm that it was Daniel's signature and one of the guards brought a book in which all the Royal guards including, past and present had signed. Caster looked both the signatures and declared that the signature matches.

"Signature can be copied, couldn't it", marked Grant.

Caster agreed and then he asked Larry that if he had anything else to prove his brother innocent. He requested to call that people whose name had been mentioned. Caster thought what to do, the evidence pointed to Daniel and Agnes but anyway he first called out the name of Oliver and Hilda. First Oliver came and he stood on the witness box with an oath and told about his last meeting with Daniel. He was asking about Eric Dunber and he told him, what he knows about him. Then Hilda came and she told the same thing, what Oliver said. This raised a question that why Daniel was so curious to know about Eric Dunber but that doesn't prove him innocent. Still, Caster became curious; he also wanted to know the truth behind the letter.

He talked with the Cardinal and the other Earls and they decided to call all the persons, whose name was mentioned the letter. Alister and Olivia were very confident that Daniel and Agens were the murderers and they also had support from other three Earls. Then the three chefs, who were best friend with their chief, were called. Their names were not mentioned but still but they understood that it was them and moved forward. The King recognized them and they accepted that they were close to their chief chef and he always tells them, whenever he goes to meet Harrison. After their statement everyone was shocked, one thing from the letter was now true and then they said that the night he was murdered, he had went to met Harrison and he was sure.

"Do you think Daniel would have killed your chief?" asked Caster.

"No, we don't know", one of them replied, "as far as we know Daniel, he was not close to us and our head chef didn't even mentioned anything about him while we talked." And other tow nodded and supported his statement.

"Then why did he kill him?"

"I don't know." "I also don't know." "Me neither and yes he was with Harrison, most of the time."

There statement gave some hope for the Trotters and now the only person remained was Princess Evelyn. Alister and her mother protested but Caster suggested that she was the only person who can prove that the letter was false, and then everything would be clear. Then they both agreed and Olivia declared punishing the Trotters for making the false letter story. The Trotters got scared because this was not what they expected. The Princess was called and she was asked about Daniel's last talk. She immediately told everything and that startled everyone.

"What are you talking?" said her father.

She was speechless.

"Are you telling the truth?" asked Castor.

"Yes, Lord Castor. I have no reason to lie."

Her statement proved that Eric Dunber was not responsible for that incident when Princess was lost. It was Harrison and that proved that the letter was true and as for the knife in Daniel's chamber, they considered that Harrison must have kept it. Alister was shaken and blamed Oliver and Hilda for teaming up but they didn't know each other. Hilda had her own witness that was Eva and her fellow servants and Oliver's witness was his master, Lord Anton. Anton was supporting the King and he had to be truth and he told that Oliver was always with him, all the time.

Lord Castor laughed that finally, someone got justice. The Trotters were very happy that Daniel and Agnes are now innocent but still, there was one more thing left. It was the King. Now people were angry that he was responsible not only to kill two innocent people but three people. The third person was Eric. The stood up as if they want to riot and Alister was in shock. Errol told that they will announce tomorrow and dismissed the trial. Next morning they all gathered again to hear the announcement.

"My dear citizens, today is the day, when all here the truth of our decision", said Errol. "We declared that Daniel Ewart and Agnes and Eric Dunber were innocent... and we declare Harrison responsible. And as for our King, his actions were perspective. He did not know what he was doing? It was all because of Harrison whom we trusted and thought to be a good person. We are very regretful that three innocent lives were lost in our presence. We can now, only pray for those innocent souls, for the safe way to heaven and make sure this won't happen again."

Larry and her father returned home happily and told the rest of the family about it. Then the whole family dressed very well and went to the village church for a wedding ceremony to attend. The wedding ceremony was of Daniel and Agnes. When the fire took over the hut, they got nowhere to run. Go out get killed, stay still get killed. They felt the heat of the fire.

"Daniel, thank you for showing the truth", she said, sadly.

"No, I'm sorry that my oath to be a guard went wasted."

"I wished we could have stayed together forever but now I wish if someone could bury us side by side", she said, sobbing.

"I wished that too."

They hugged each other. The fire heat was stronger and Daniel felt it on his face and recalled, he thought about how Wilson helped him and then the Trotters and then the Princess came and he saved her and then he was rewarded and then he went to become the Royal guard and then... Suddenly something struck on Daniel mind and he remembered that he hadn't taken the reward out from the house. He moved and the fire rampaged over the roof top and it almost fell on Agnes. She screamed.

Daniel pulled her away from the fire and then he moved his bed aside and opened the secret closet which Wilson had built for keeping things safe. He opened it and jumped in and found the two hundred gold coins reward was in it. The walls started to collapse and Agnes screamed again. The closet was actually a tunnel naturally built beneath it, maybe by a hare a long time ago. Daniel left his sword behind and they both went under and crawled out from the backside of the hut. The King and his men were on the front side of the house and didn't notice them escaping.

They ran to the Trotter's resident. Lewis opened the door and was surprised seeing them. Later in the morning, Daniel explained everything about the incident and how they ended up running. The Trotter never doubted his words and they helped to gather things so that they could flee to England and it took few days. Later by the customers, they learnt everyone was thinking that they were innocent and a trial was going to be prepared for them to ensure that they were criminals.

After thinking a lot, they decided to remain dead but still wanted to punish the dead Harrison. And so Daniel made a plan and explained Larry and his father who could help them out and then they joined the trial because Daniel trusted the Princess would help them and so she did. He also wrote a letter explaining this and that. And in the end, everything moved on according to their plan except for the death threaten from the King's mother, which was unexpected.

Except for the Trotters, no one else participated in their wedding and the priest, if counted. The priest declared them as husband and wife. Then Daniel placed a pair of shoes on the grave of Wilson as a token of thank you. Mr. Trotter returned the sword which he left behind when he went to train to become the Royal guard. Then he and Mrs. Ewart fled to their new life while Alister became very depressed. It was very tough for him to believe that his childhood friend betrayed him. In the end, he resigned from the throne because now he was in the condition that he could trust no one.

-Charles E. Ekka

2. Captain Croc

A passenger ship named White Falcon was one day away from reaching the port of Swansea when it was attacked by two pirate ships. The watch sailor of the White Falcon mistook them for merchant ships from Spain and France which was actually a disguise. Before he could discover about it, it was too late. They fired cannons, broke down the masts, jumped on their ship and killed those who tried to resist and anchored it.

Both the pirate ships were commanded by a pirate Captain named Morgan Hilton. He was also known as Death Wave, given by the sailors for his brutality. He killed innocent and hanged the head of his enemy pirate or a Marine on his ship. He was one of the most feared pirates with a bounty of over five hundred thousand pounds, from four European nations. Beside he commanded a fleet of twenty-one pirate ships, who shared one-third of their loot and he considers himself to be above everyone.

The survived crew members of White Falcon were captured and gathered on the main deck, while the passengers were taken to the ballroom of the ship. Morgan came and he looked to the White Falcon's crew. All were terrified and their Captain was not with them. His name was Captain Bloom. When the pirates fired cannons, he was having lunch with a lady passenger, whom he met on the main deck. One of cannons hit into his cabin but they were not injured. When he was about to go to fight the pirates, the lady got so terrified that she did not let him go and he was stuck with her.

They heard and felt the destruction done by cannons and then they heard screaming of people. Somehow, Bloom insisted her, to let him go and suggested her to stay in the cabin. He walked to the door and as he touched the door knob, he heard someone running to his cabin, and then heard a gunshot and his running crewmate fell near the door. He had slightly opened it and saw him falling. He immediately closed the door and hid the lady in his wardrobe. Four pirates were searching for him and they found him by the name board on the door.

"The Captain is here", said one of the pirates.

They broke into the cabin and found the Captain. Bloom surrendered himself, thinking that he could protect the lady but he was wrong. The pirates were here to loot and two of them found the lady when they searched the wardrobe for valuable things.

"Leave her, you have me", protested Bloom.

They didn't listen and took them on the main deck where Morgan was waiting for him.

"Captain, we found the Captain."

By the time, the pirates were looting things from the lockers, kitchen, passenger cabin and anything valuable and were carrying it to their ships. Then another pirate search party came with a crew member.

"Captain, this is the last crew of this ship. He was hiding in the ladies bathroom."

Bloom looked to his fellow crewmate. He was his nephew and was terrified and there was also the frightened lady passenger too. He quickly thought of some strategy to negotiate.

"I want to speak with your Captain", demanded Bloom.

"Aye, what you want to talk?" replied Morgan, coming close to him.

"You can take whatever you want, just let my crew and the passengers go. And if you want to kill me, then kill me and please, spare the others."

"I'm already taking what I want and as for sparing the others? If I spare them, then how could I scare the civilians and my enemies and if I do, they will think that I'm soft hearted and I don't want them to think like that."

"Please, I'm begging you, don't do this, they are innocent. They have done nothing wrong against you."

"I know", he replied.

Morgan gave a hand signal to one of his men and he nodded. They pushed Bloom and his nephew to the ship's side edge and emptied their pockets. The young crewmate sobbed and Bloom felt pity and guilty because he was the one who encouraged him to become a sailor. Then he turned down to the sea and he was shocked. All the rest of his ship's crew members were bleeding dead in the sea. First, they cut the throat of the Captain and then of the young man and threw them into the sea. Like this Morgan makes the sea water red, as his symbol that he was here and everyone should fear him.

The lady passenger hopelessly watched and sobbed and then she was taken and thrown among the other passengers in the ballroom. One of Morgan's crew mates bought a chair and placed it on one side of the ballroom. It was for Morgan. He sat on it and ordered the passengers to surrender all the money and jewellery they had. They made a queue and placed all their goods in the sack, kept on the floor, one by one. Then a passenger surrendered all her money and jewellery and as she was going back Morgan stopped her.

"Hey women, I said to surrender all your money and jewellery", reminded Morgan in a harsh tone.

"I have given everything", she replied, terrified.

Morgan stood up from his chair and walked to her. "Women, do I look blind", he said. She couldn't reply. "Hand over me your ring."

"No, I can't", moving two steps away and it took everyone's attention.

"Hand over it, it is mine now", he demanded.

"No, I can't. This is my engagement ring from my future husband."

"Hand it over!"

She shook her head no, holding her hands.

"Please, I'm begging you", she said, sobbing.

"Fine then", Morgan took out his gun and shot her, on the head. It scared the passengers, especially the children. They caught their parents tightly and sobbed. Morgan removed the ring her finger.

"Don't worry about your future husband, he will marry someone else. This is what most of the people do", he commented.

Two of his men took her dead body and the lady who was with Bloom saw her very closely and imagined herself that it could be her too. They tossed the women's dead body into the sea while other pirates were still transporting goods to their ships. Then one of the pirates who threw the dead women saw a ship on the horizon to the South-West. It looked familiar. There was a pirate, who was holding a telescope and he took it from him and looked through it. He was stunned. It was another pirate ship, an enemy pirate. The other pirate also looked and he got the same reaction. They both immediately went to the ballroom and immediately informed their Captain. Morgan was shocked. He looked to him.

"Are you sure?" he asked.

He nodded, "Aye Captain, or kill me if false."

Morgan quickly thought to take a decision walked around "What happened?" asked a crew mate to another.

"You will know soon."

Morgan took a deep breath and then turned to them and announced, "My fellow victims, I think God and the devil hate all of you and they don't want me to send you all to heaven or hell. So ladies and gentlemen, suffer in the world with your riches. Until we meet again", to the passengers. "Okay everyone aboard the ship!" to his men.

They all left and went to their respective ships and all were informed about the enemy pirate ship and they set their sails. They were after a ship called Ocean Jaw which was commanded by a fearless pirate Captain named Croc. His ship front part was shaped like a crocodile head and decks and edges look like the scales of a lizard. Since the day, Morgan witnessed and saw Ocean Jaw crushing through a Spanish merchant ship without getting damaged, like he had heard the rumours about it; he wanted to capture it. Once he was close, but he missed and now it was the second time and he doesn't want to lose it again.

After several hours of sailing, the Ocean Jaw ship slowed down and anchored. Morgan and his first mate, Josh, who was commanding Morgan's other ship, were little amazed, but that didn't stop them from pursuing their attack. Ocean Jaw's crew was watching and they were stationed to fire the cannons for the fight. First Morgan's ships fired and from both sides and the Ocean Jaw got caught in the middle of their attack. They got no chance to fire the cannons and after a while, Morgan and his crew took over the Ocean Jaw with creating less damage.

Almost all of them got on the deck of Ocean Jaw and they tied the crew members along the masts, who surrendered. Morgan's crew was very happy, shouting and celebrating their achievement.

Morgan kissed the deck's floor. "Finally love, you are mine", he said.

The ship damaged part repaired magically and some of the pirates got terrified but Morgan didn't. He became delighted that he had captured something precious than gold.

"Don't be afraid my mates, this magical ship is ours now, and with this, sailing by our side, no one can ever stop us!" he said and everybody's confident was awakened and they cheered out loud.

He and a few of his men charged into the Captain's cabin. It was dark, except for one candle light on the table, where Croc was drinking wine as if nothing had happened. Morgan sat on the chair in front of him and one of his men took the wine bottle and drunk it.

"Wow, Wow, it's good, it's good, no no it's very best wine that I have ever consumed. What's this? What is the name of the wine, fellow?" he asked Croc but he didn't reply.

"It's only me and the Captain!" declared Morgan and his men became silent.

"Are you here for my gold...? How should I address you, Captain..." said Croc, calmly.

"It's Morgan, Captain Morgan... or you can call me Death Wave, like the cowards, who gave me this code name... and it's not bad, it suits me."

"So Captain Morgan, are you here for my gold? You can have it. It is below the deck."

"Gold, that's my favourite thing but actually I'm here to offer you something", Croc looked directly into his eyes. "Join my fleet, and give me one-third of your loot. We would be unstoppable and we will rule the sea."

"Rule the sea? You mean you will rule the sea", considered Croc.

"Of course, I'm the leader of my fleet and you will be joining it."

Croc paused for a second and replied, "I refuse."

Morgan hates when a person refuses his demand like women in the White Falcon ship. He sighed and they were silent for a moment. Then he saw a book on the side of the table. It was a Bible. He picked it up carelessly and tore a piece of a page from it.

"Oh, forgive me Lord that I tore a part of you. Hope you can heal yourself because you are the God, who can perform miracles for your sinned children and why not on himself?"

"God will forgive you", said Croc.

"It seemed like you are a Christian", he said.

Croc remained silent and gazed him, emptying the wine cup, completely. Morgan sighed, stood up and took out his gun.

"There is something that I don't understand... that why some people like you love to die, when they get a chance to live? I guess not all life is blessed beautiful as it seemed... but don't worry, I'll spare your crew if they agree to work for me."

"Sorry, but what crew are you talking about? I don't have a crew."

Morgan thought he must be trying to distract him and it was not a good distraction. He pointed his gun at him and Croc stayed still.

"Now I understood, why people love to die... because death doesn't cheat them like life does", he said. "Still, it takes courage to love death and I hope you have that courage... any last word."

"Hope, you have the courage of getting wet", replied Croc.

Morgan and his men didn't understand his statement, but as he pulled the trigger, the whole ship disappeared along with Croc. Morgan and all his men, who were on the deck of Ocean Jaw, fell into the sea. It startled everyone and they wondered what the heck just happened? It was not like every day when you see a whole ship vanished right in front of naked eyes. Morgan somehow swam over the water and almost all of his men were struggling to stay above the water.

"Ocean Jaw is over there!" Someone from Morgan's ship cried.

He turned and saw the ship. At the same time, the back door of the Ocean Jaw was opened and ten salt water crocodiles came out and swum towards them.

"Cro-Crocodiles! Climb on the ship! Climb on the ship!" cried the same person.

The crocodiles came and attacked them. Morgan somehow managed to climb on one of his ships without getting harmed and the crocodiles kept on eating his men. He ordered to bring rifles and they brought and aimed for the crocodiles. It was very hard to get a clear shot, but they fired and accidently, they shot four of their own men. Morgan saw his first mate, Josh was getting eaten. He fired a shot and it strikes the crocodile. But one shot had no effect on it and the crocodile ate Josh, leaving his right hand, floating.

Two crocodiles jaw got stuck on the net from which all of them were climbing on the ship. They pulled and broken it down and the men on the net fell back on the sea. They all were eaten and the sea water turned red. Morgan hopelessly watched, angrily. He was frustrated and ran to the other edge of his ship and fired bullets at Ocean Jaw. Croc simply watched him. Then the crocodiles returned back to his ship and they sailed away. Some of his survived men's legs were eaten and they were grunting on the deck and others were waiting for his orders. He made himself calm and observed the situation. He ordered his men to sail back, but soon after the order, four English Marines warships arrived.

There were five English warships patrolling and they came across to the collapsed White Falcon. One of the ships helped the passengers and sailed them towards their destination, while the other four sailed towards the South-West. One of the passengers from White Falcon saw in which direction those pirates were going and he told the Marines. They had a small crossfire fight and the pirates lost. Morgan and twenty-five of his men surrendered and they were taken to Portsmouth and imprisoned. There were also other pirates too, who were waiting for their trial, which was a death sentence.

* * *

John Bowen arrived at a restaurant, at Winchester. He was a Marine inspector in English Marines. His work was to investigate and search the details about pirates like where they are from? Or where they live? Who else work for them? And to get their face sketch.

He asked the restaurant manager that if he knew a person named Harry Smith. The manager agreed that a person with that name works in his restaurant as a waiter and he summoned him. He was an average looking person. He was taken to the back side of the restaurant and John asked him about his abduction details by a pirate named Croc and also warned him that if he tried to defend him or make any stories, he will be charged for treason against his country for supporting a pirate and worse thing could happen to him that he will be convicted death sentence.

It was not more than ten years since Croc showed up as a pirate Captain. The day he defeated Isaac Rochussen a pirate Captain and his fleet of fifty of pirate ships and soon after Phillip Ras, another pirate Captain and his fleet of a thirty-eight pirate ship, he became famous among everyone. He looted several other passenger ships and merchant ships and he was seen in many parts of the world. Many European Marines along with other countries claimed that they had killed that pirate, but soon after a few days, sailors see him sailing on his ship and sometime he will be with his fleets and even get attacked by him. And that led to make people believe that he had supernatural powers to control the sea and the most terrifying power was that he comes back to life.

And as for John, he had a different theory, still with doubts. After five years of hard work, John finally found a lead in his investigation and that was Harry Smith. John asked him few questions which Harry answered it, fluently and then he returned to Portsmouth. When he arrived at the Marine headquarter, he learnt that two days ago a most wanted pirate named Morgan Hilton and some of his crew members were caught and they had encountered Croc. He immediately went to the prison and saw them cuffed along with other prisoners.

"Did you questioned him about the rest of his fleet?" asked John, to a prison guard, who was with him.

"No, Chief Admiral Walker had strictly instructed not to question him and let him have his court trial", replied the guard.

"Court trial? Why would he decide that?"

"Because Admiral believes that he may appeal for a deal and the deal could be to set him free, instead of the name and location of his fleet. And he could walk free. And Admiral Walker doesn't want this to happen."

"Admiral had a point... and what about his men? Do they too have to wait for the trial?"

"He never mentioned anything about them?"

John got the opportunity. He took one of the pirates from Morgan's crew with four prison guards to a separate chamber where he questioned him about Croc. He didn't reply. Then he asked him harshly.

"Go to hell", said the pirate.

John felt that there was no point to question a pirate, nicely. He tortured him with a hot iron rode by contacting it on the pirate's leg, several times. The pirate screamed in pain and finally, he broke down and at last, he spoke and told every detail about his encountering with Croc. After that, he went to meet the Admirals, who caught Morgan. One of them was Admiral Allen. He met him at his house and they talked about, how they caught Morgan Hilton and what was the scenario? Then John went to meet the Chief Admiral Walker. He told him about the details that he had gathered about Croc and he requested to arrange a meeting with the alliance for information sharing. Walker agreed and started to prepare the meeting. John returned home where his beautiful wife and his pretty little daughter were waiting for him for a long time.

"Daddy is home, mommy", said her daughter and she ran and her father hugged her tightly with joy.

He was away for almost five years. The longest time he was away from his family. His wife also came running and tears of joy came down from her eyes and they hugged, happily.

Meanwhile, at Winchester a person came, late night at Harry Smith's door. Harry opened the door and found that it was Croc. He let him in and they sat at the dining table.

"You wrote that someone came to meet you?" asked Croc.

"Yes, his name was John Bowen. He is a Marine inspector. I don't know how he did, but he reached for me and he was asking questions about you."

Croc took out a blank paper and a pencil and asked Harry to draw his face.

"Are you joking? You know I cannot draw", he replied.

"Just draw", he ordered, looking into his eyes.

Harry took the pencil and paper and drew the face of John Bowen exactly as if he was a master artist. Croc took the sketch and looked it.

"So this is him", said Croc.

"Any new order, Captain?" asked Harry.

Croc looked to him and took the pencil from his hand.

"Your work is already complete and my purpose is fulfilled. It's time I should return it", he replied and walked out of the house. "Farewell, first mate."

Harry forgot everything that he was ever related to Croc. Croc erased all his memories related to him.

* * *

Three weeks later, Marine officers from four different countries arrived at the headquarters in Portsmouth in their fleet of warships. Vice Admiral Mora from Spain with his Lieutenant, Captain and Commander Vane from France with his junior Lieutenant, Admiral Baker from Norway with his high ranking officer and many other English Captains, Commanders and Lieutenants gathered in the hall. France, Norway, Spain and England's political relationship were not good, but since their enemy was common and in large number, they had made as an alliance.

"Good morning everyone, I Chief Admiral Walker of the English Marines, warmly welcome you all the foreign Marine officers, for this information sharing meeting and thank you all for arriving at the given time", he said and then he introduced John, "And my fellow Marines, this is John Bowen, he is a Marine Inspector and he will explain you everything for our meeting."

Walker went to his seat and John said, "Okay, let's get to the topic. So, we are here to share information about the pirate who goes by the name Croc. That's so far we know about his name."

"Croc, but sir..." said Admiral Baker. "And sorry to interrupt, our Marine had killed that pirate and his fleet, a year ago and I know we have sent the report to the alliance, about him."

Everyone was puzzled, but John replied, "Oh... I remember. I had read that report. It was the second time, I was reading... but Admiral I think the pirate group which your Marine force killed must be one of his copycats."

"Copycats?" some of them muttered.

"What do you mean by copycats?" asked a Marine.

"I will say that soon... but first I want to discuss something else about him. So we have heard many rumours, like his ship repairs itself, even after it was hit by hundreds of cannon, he shows no mercy, he doesn't sleep at all, he eats the human flesh and a lot more... but one rumour we have heard and we most of them believed, that is, he can come back to life", he explained.

"So, is it true then?" asked a junior Marine.

"Well, no. It isn't", he answered.

"Any evidence?" asked Vane.

"Yes", he said and went to the table where he had kept a bunch of files. He picked some of the files and he handed it to them. "And please be careful, I only got one copy of it. Thank you."

They glanced over each of the files. It had faces sketch drawing of different pirates from many countries, like China, Japan, North Africa, North and South America and some of the European countries and all of them were named to be Croc with signatures and thumbprints, below. They had taken his name only to terrorize and loot. Admiral Walker was also stunned after seeing so many faces thought he had seen a few of them.

"If a person, come back to like, I don't think, he will change his face all the time, or even his gender", he said, two of the sketches were of a female pirate, who had disguised as a male pirate, Croc.

"Hmm... this is, indeed, something new", marked Vane.

"Nice work, Bowen", greeted Walker.

"Thank you, Chief."

"One question?" said Vane. "Do you have his face sketch? I mean the real face of Croc."

"Unfortunately, no, I don't have his real face sketch", said John.

No one got anything to say. Most of them expected that he had finally had his sketch for a second.

"But I have a way to find him", claimed John.

"Okay, you don't have his face sketch, then what about his crew", interrupted Vane. "Some civilians must have survived their attack and anyone could have remembered, one of his crew mate's faces."

"I don't have their sketches either... but I learnt about a person through a civilian, who heard him talking about Croc and believed to be one of Croc's crew, but after investigation and talking with him, he turned out to be an ordinary citizen", replied John.

"So, in other words, we are empty-handed, I mean it's been over eight or nine years since he was creating terror in the sea", said Vane.

"Don't forget fellow Admiral, he is not the only pirate we had faced and besides we learnt that he doesn't come back to life. There were copycats of him", interrupted Admiral Mora.

"Oh, Yes, I know", he replied, calmly.

"So what were you saying earlier, you said you have a way to find him?" remained Walker.

John explained that there are two types of survivors who encountered Croc, one who saw the face of Croc but later forgot and those who saw and helped the Marines to draw his sketch. The people who saw his face and Croc's sketch was made were actually turned out to be copycats, as mostly they were described in the files which he had already presented to them. Those who don't remember his face was the actual issue and they had one thing in common, most of them. They worked on merchant ships which were from Spain and all of them were owned by the Duke of Cadiz, Elias Leonor.

He handed over the files where the survived merchant sailors, work detail, a statement about encountering with the Croc and their master's name, that was Elias Leonor was written with the signature and everybody glanced over it, one by one.

"So you want to say that the real identity of Croc is this Duke", guessed a young Marine.

"No, if he was a pirate then why would he be sinking his own ship."

"So you mean he is related to him, somehow", marked the French Lieutenant.

"Yes, that's what I think. And one more thing, we have uncovered one rumour that he come back to life, but I believe that not every rumour is false. Some of them might be true, like in this case. There are dangerous pirates whose face sketch we got within two months and over a year maybe, but we are having difficult to find this pirate's sketch because no one remembers, how he looks... which mean, he must have some kind of ability that makes people forget his face." Everyone assumed in their thoughts that John was right at some point. "Oh, I almost forgot", he continued. "Recently, three weeks ago, our Marines caught a most wanted pirate named Morgan Hilton and some of his crew, who is charged with mass homicide, looting and many other pirate crimes which is usual for a pirate. Then I learnt that he and his crew had encountered Croc and because of some issues, I was not allowed to question the pirate Captain, but I talked with one of his crew mates, which was not easy, but he said that they almost won against Croc and then... the ship vanished and when it reappeared, it sets loose crocodiles and it ate almost all of his crew mates. The Ocean Jaw ship sailed away and then we Marines arrive and after... a fight he was caught."

"Sir, I believe that he must be having some kind of ability to make people forgot, but ship vanishing, crocodiles, this thinks puts back to the place where we uncovered that he does not resurrect."

"Yes, I know, but I have a witness present here.... He is a high ranking officer. Let me introduce, Admiral Allen, he was there when they arrested Hilton."

Allen stood up from his seat and he told that he was patrolling the sea with five of his ships when they found a passenger ship, looted by pirates. One of the passengers had seen in which direction the pirates went and how many ships they were having. Leavening one ship for the passengers they went with four and when they found them, they had a fight but it didn't last long. When they surrendered, they found some pirate's legs were chopped and lying in the cabin and some were dead, floating on the sea, but they were not killed by the Marine cannons but eaten by a sea creature and they told him like John said now. And all the pirates whose legs were chopped, died while bringing them to Portsmouth because of infection.

"Pardon me, sir, but what kind of creatures, are they sharks", asked a young Marine officer to Admiral Allen.

"Not sharks, they were crocodiles... and I also mentioned in my previous statement", explained John, interrupting.

"Yes, that is it", said Allen.

"Thank you for your statement, Admiral", said John and he sat back in his seat.

There was a silence for a moment.

"Did you gather all this information by yourself?" asked Vane.

"No. There were ten of us, including me and six of them died while gathering the information."

The Marines felt sympathy for his fallen subordinates.

"And did you talk to the Duke?" asked Mora.

"No, I haven't. I got no time for that", answered John. "But I'll sail as soon as I can and I'll send the report to each alliance... and before we dismiss our meeting, let me show you the last report of my... I mean our investigation."

John unrolled and hung a sketch drawing of a ship on the board, whose front was shaped like a crocodile and the side edges were like the scales of a lizard.

"This is the ship which Croc commands and it is called Ocean Jaw... not a perfect portrait but the artist has drawn as the people described it and they were the one who doesn't remember his face."

That picture startled everyone because no one had even seen that kind of pirate ship and when John asked if anyone had encountered it, there reply was no.

"So officers... this is all I had to share from the investigation. Thank you for coming."

Everybody left the hall and John collected all the files which he handed them. Later, John was summoned to Walker's office where the Spanish Marines, Admiral Mora and his Lieutenant were also present. It was actually Mora who wanted to meet him. He was very impressed by his presentation of his latest investigation which he just shared and since he will continue his further investigation after few weeks, he asked him to hand over the evidence to the Spanish Marine and let them continue the investigation. Walker was supporting the suggestion, but John refused. He doesn't want to handover, the reason of the death of his subordinate just like that; he wanted to investigate by himself.

"Okay, if you don't want to hand over them, what about working with our Marine inspector by your side?" said Mora.

John thought for a moment.

"Well... that's a great idea", he answered.

"Then you have to come with us. We are leaving tomorrow."

"No, I can't."

"You should Bowen; the longer we will wait, the further we will get away from Croc. This is our chance to catch him soon and bring him to justice."

John decided to go with them. He returned home and told his wife about it. She wasn't delighted by his decision because he had told her that he would be staying for five months and now he was leaving within two months. She was very worried about him. She always prayed for his safe returned every single day when he was out at work for five years. Somehow, John convinced her and promised that this will be his last work and he will retire from Marines after he was done with his work. She felt a little relief and said that she will pray for him every evening in the church which made John happy that she cares him a lot and so does he, for her and his beloved daughter.

John packed all the stuffs which he needed, including his sword and next morning he set sail with the Spanish Marines. The Spanish soldiers made fun of him by speaking in Spanish, but he shut them up by speaking in Spanish. John was half Spanish. His mother was from Spain. That very day when John Bowen left for Spain that morning, Hilton Morgan and his crew were presented in the court for the trial, where they were convicted guilty with many illegal and murder charges and declared the death penalty for him and his crew by tomorrow.

Some passengers from White Falcon including the lady, who was with Captain Bloom, were also present in the court and they gave their statement, on their hostage situation.

"Yes, exactly, this is what you should get for killing Bloom!" said the lady. But the pirates remained silent and some of the passengers.

"You devil, there no place on earth for you, soon you will burn in hell!"

"Wish I would be the one to pull the lever to hang you!"

"If I want I will...!"

"Silence in court!" interrupted the judge. "This is a courtroom, not a public place", then he turned to the pirates, "as for our country jurisdiction rule, the court gives you a chance to speak. Would anyone of you like to speak anything in your defence?"

They remained silent and then the judge asked them again.

"Defence... oh yes, I would like to say that... bail me and my crew mates. Bail us permanently and give us a ship or a boat. We will sail away peacefully... without killing you and your family", said Morgan to the judge.

The judge got furious and he ordered the guards to take them away and through them back into that dirty prison cell. The passengers of White Falcon felt happy and relief that Morgan will be hanged. Finally, they are about to get justice. In the evening, the judge returned home and found that the main door was opened. He walked inside calling the name of his wife and children. When he walked into the dining room, he was stunned. He found his wife and three daughters were killed. They were beheaded and their body was seated on the chair and heads were on the table. The judge got terrified and started sobbing. Somebody patted his shoulder. He turned and saw a tall man smiling at him. Then four more men came out of the room with guns and swords, one of the swords was stained with blood and the person, holding it, was cleaning it with a dress of his little daughter.

"So he arrived", said a female voice.

She came down from the stairs. Her name was Freya and she was the lover of Morgan Hilton and she was a witch. They all were present during the court trial.

"Why? Why? What have I done to you?" said the judge, sobbing.

"Because our Captain ordered us", one of them replied.

They were also present in the court when he charged the pirates. The judge fell on his knees and sobbed.

"Kill him", said Freya and they killed him in the same manner as they killed his family members.

Then they went to the prison, where their Captain and some of his crew mates were imprisoned. Freya used her magical spells and put every guard who was present on their way into deep sleep. She went with two men while the other three waited outside, with public carriages. They found the keys from one of the prison guard's belt, hanging and broke their comrades out and they were very happy to see each other. As they got out of the prison cell, the other prisoners begged them to set them free too. Morgan thought for a second and dropped the key, away from their cell.

"Help yourself", he said, "pigs."

And they ran out.

The prisoners stretched out their hands of their cell bars, to reach the keys but it was far anyway. Then one of the prisoners rolled his shirt and threw its one end to the keys. The keys got trapped among the shirt's strings in one throw and he pulled it back, gently. They set themselves free. Still, there were other prisoners in other cells and they also begged them to set them free, but the prisoners who were free now showed the same manner like Morgan. They dropped the keys and ran out. But it was their bad luck that they all were caught by the guards under the gunpoint and were brought back to the same cell from where they escaped, a few second ago, while Morgan and his entire crew, silently ran outside the prison boundary, sat in the three carriages and rode to the shore. From there they sat on three boats which were brought to his crew who rescued them and climbed on their ship and escaped in the night wave.

* * *

After five days of sailing, John arrived at the port of Cadiz. He looked the house near the ports. They were very beautiful. He thought of spending the vacation with his family. Before parting with John, Mora gave him a coupon of a hotel which he owned and instructed that they will send their Marine inspector to the hotel. John took the token and walked on his way. He took a carriage to the hotel and showed the token at the counter. He got a room in free. He became fresh, ate his breakfast at the hotel's restaurant and waited for the Spanish Marine inspector to arrive.

Later, he went to have lunch and again waited for him, but he did not arrive. In the evening, a Marine soldier came to his hotel room and told him that the inspector, who was supposed to work with him was sick and don't know when he will be healed and Admiral Mora had requested him to wait for three more days. But John didn't want to wait. He decided to work alone. Next morning, he took the things which he needed in a bag and went to the Duke's house in a carriage. It was a long ride, but he reached, without any problem.

He asked the carriage rider to wait for him and he walked to the gate. He found that there were no gate guards, and there was no one inside the boundary. He walked inside through a small gate and walked to the door. The house was very quiet like nobody lived there. He knocked and after a long moment a person responded. It was a butler.

"How can I help you, sir?" he asked.

"My name is John Bowen and I'm from England. I'm a Marine inspector and I want to meet the Duke", he replied.

"Marine inspector..."

John showed his identity card to him and the butler looked it carefully.

"Does my master know about your arrival?"

"No, I just arrived yesterday."

"What is the work with him?"

"I'm on an investigation. I'm here to talk about a pirate Croc..."

"Croc... this pirate who sank my master's ship?" he interrupted.

"Yes, it was Croc."

The butler excused and went inside to talk with his master. After a moment, he returned and asked him to come inside and gave him to sit in the living room. John felt awkward, the living room was almost empty with furniture and carpets, except on which he was seated and the walls had frame marks and the house was very quiet, like it was deserted. Then Elias the Duke came and he stood up and bowed to him.

"Good afternoon, Your Grace, and thank you for giving time to meet me", he greeted.

"Good afternoon", replied the Duke and he sat facing opposite to him and the butler stood by him. "I heard you want to talk about the pirate who sank my ships."

"Yes Your Grace", replied John, blissfully.

"So how can I help you?"

John explained by showing him some papers which contained the detail list of sixty ships from which twenty merchant ships first belonged to the Duke and they were looted by the same pirate four times in a year and then it was sunk with him. Then fifteen new merchant ships were bought by the Duke again and the fate ended with the same tragedy and in the coming days he rented many other ships and they also met the same fate as the previous ships.

"You have a very good detail of my lost ships. It costs a lot of money", marked Elias. "I guess you have come to Spain many times."

"Actually, it was one of my subordinates who came to Spain and collected the details of the ships attacked by pirates from the harbour."

"So where is he now? Your co-worker or whatever you call your officers?"

"Dead... during a sea voyage. He was attacked by a pirate though few people on that ship survived. He came here only to collect the details of the ships that turned out some of them were yours."

"Hmm... no one knows who will die and that happened with my father."

"Sorry for your loss."

"Croc", interrupted Elias with astonishment. "This bastard is responsible for everything that I lost."

"Yes, he is."

"Good, he was killed by Norwegian Marines, and these Spanish Marines... oh couldn't do a small work... I don't know why the King pays them money for..."

"Actually, he is not dead and the Norwegian Marines actually killed one of his copycats. There were pirates who were pretending to be him", explained John. "And during my investigation I learnt that the actual Croc had attacked only your merchant ships."

Elias became silent for a moment and then looked to John.

"If you are correct, why is he doing this to me? And what the hell happened to Spanish Marines? Cannot take down a pirate... the Marine force was great when I was their commander, what the hell happened to them now? Seemed like the new one is not serious of his position... Or do you think something or some type of conspiracy is being plotted against me? Well... I'm going to be a King someday and I will marry the Princess. There will be someone who will be jealous of me and that bastard must have bribed that pirate to do this tragedy. But what I have done wrong to them and why they... they should be ashamed for their act and when I will become the King and caught them, they will be very regretful, very badly... Especially the new Marine commander", declared Elias.

"I don't know about the conspiracy or the bribe but I have a different opinion about him and I think he knows you. Maybe for a long time, you two know each other and that's why he is attacking your ships", said John, "as if he was offended by you, somehow."

John didn't mention about the Spanish Marines because he thought that it could put him in trouble because the Duke mentioned that he was going to be the King.

"What did you say?" and Elias and John repeated his statement and that enraged the Duke. He took it as insulting for him and burst on him. "Who the hell are you to insult me like that by connecting a relationship to a pig head pirate", John was speechless. "Do you know what I'll become in the coming days? I'll be the King of Spain. I will marry the Princess. She is the most beautiful girl in the world. How dare you to insult me?" John was still speechless. "Get out of my house! And don't come back to Spain or I will make sure you will die for the disrespect of the future King." And Elias walked away. "Make sure he walks out of the boundary!" he said to the butler from a distance.

John quickly packed his stuff and the butler walked him till the gate. John wasn't happy that his investigation was stopped by a mad Duke and situation seemed to sail back to England sooner than expected.

As he walked out of the gate, the butler said, "You can travel around Cadiz. There won't be any legal law troubling you. Have a good day, sir."

"What law are you talking about? And who is letting him marry the Princess?" he asked. "What the hell happened to him?"

The butler thought for a second and explained that the Duke was in stress for a couple of years. He had some ships from his birth rights and later he bought a few more to expand his merchant business, but then the pirate looted and sank them. Then he bought more ships and the new ships ended in the same tragedy and from that point he should have stopped, but he borrowed many ships in rent and they were also drowned. But again, he didn't stop and started hotel business which also didn't work at all.

"Why are you telling me this?"

"Because you asked..."

"Won't you be in trouble?"

"No, the loans which he had taken from many banks for the ships and hotels are very huge and he couldn't pay his guards and as for becoming the King, is way over for him, a long time ago. And soon, I will also stop working for him since he won't be able to pay me."

"So everything will become bank's property", concluded John.

"Yes, you can see the living room is quite empty... okay pardon me now", said the butler and turned to return.

John stopped him and asked him if he knows anything about Croc.

"No, I don't", replied the butler.

"Anyway, thank you", said John and started to walk to his carriage, when the butler changed his mind and asked him to stop.

"Sir", he said.

"Yes."

The butler looked around and told him an address and a name. John felt awkward but he went on that given address and it was on the outskirts of the city. He came across a house.

The name which the butler told him was none other than the Duke's mother, Alma. He came down from his carriage and walked to the door and knocked. A lady named Brisa responded the knock; she was a caretaker of Alma.

Brisa severed his tea and then Alma asked, "So what do you want to know about?"

"Well, ma'am, it's about Croc the pirate who attacks only your son's ship as if it is his personal problem. Now your son is bankrupted. Do you know anything about Croc?"

"Hmm... son, do you have parents?" asked Alma.

"Yes, ma'am", he answered.

"Do you meet them?"

"Yes, ma'am, once in a year, because of work and they live in a separate house, like you."

"Your parents must be blessed one to have you and then there is me who have a son and he had kicked me out of his house and went to become the King of Spain. How cruel? Cannot care his mother and went to serve the country."

"Well, good news for you, now he cannot. He is bankrupted and I don't think the King will repay his debts for making him next King."

"That must be terrible for him. It should be a lesson for him", she said.

"Excuse me... about my earlier question."

Alma took a long pause and said, "I was born in a rich and religious family and nearly forty years ago, my marriage was arranged by my father with a Duke, Elias's father. I thought it was a bad decision, but I was wrong. We lived in joy and had two sons. The elder one was Edgar and the younger was Elias. Both of them were adorable. Then one day while travelling back from Ireland, my husband's merchant ship was attacked by a pirate ship and he was on it. They won the fight against the pirate, but my husband was killed. Since then, I raised the two boys by myself and when they grow up they both joined the Marines to fight pirates as an honour to their father. After few years, Edgar received a higher position almost like his father. Then one day we are invited to the Royal party where the King saw something in Edgar and he talked with me that someday he could be a great King as he didn't have a son for his reign but a daughter. When I told Edgar about it, he didn't like it, but Elias became jealous. Elias wanted to marry the Princess and wanted to become the King instead but that was not possible. Then one day when they were patrolling in the sea of Ireland and while returning my evil young son drugged Edgar and sets him on a boat during a pirate ambush and told me that he was killed. I lived in agony... for very long. The King gave my son, Elias the title of Duke, but never said they will give their daughter's hand.... I couldn't believe it that I lost my son. I prayed all day that it was a false story. I became a mad woman and my son kicked me out on the street. I wandered around the street in madness for five months, but one day a miracle happened. My prayers were heard and my son Edgar found me. He was alive and had become a fine man."

"But ma'am, I want to know about Croc. If..." then he realized. "Wait a moment... you have an elder son, Edgar and he was left on the sea... he is the Croc... the pirate which I'm hunting for a long time. Now everything makes a scene. Elias left Edgar in the sea and somehow Edgar survived and became pirates and only looted his brother's ship and make him bankrupt for revenge", then he also realized, "and he must be visiting you, here or else you will be still on the street", concluded John.

"Please leave Edgar alone. He hasn't killed any innocent", requested Alma.

"Sorry ma'am, but a pirate is a pirate. And it is my duty to bring him to justice", he replied. As he stood up to go he saw the photo of a person and below his name was written, Love Edgar.

"Is that him?" he asked the caretaker and she nodded.

He took the photo and returned to his hotel room. In one day everything was done so quickly without the help of the Spanish inspector. He started to write the report of his investigation and decided to meet Mora to tell him that he now knew how Croc looks like and what is his real identity and where he always visits, casually. He took a deep breath and relaxed, the work was finally over for him.

As he stood up, to go to have dinner, he heard a scream of a woman. He took his sword and ran down to the lobby and found a woman sitting and few people had gathered around her including the hotel manager.

"What happened?" John asked the manager.

"A pirate abducted her son", he replied, "and her husband and some men have run after him."

"Which direction did they go?" asked John.

"I think to the harbour", said one person.

Without thinking anything he also ran out to help. He found a carriage parked beside the road and asked him to go to the harbour. The carriage rode at its maximum speed. On the way, John wondered that why a pirate would abduct a child from the middle of the city? They arrived and the carriage left him at a distance away from the harbour. He told the rider to wait and he went walking. The harbour was very quiet and he found some horses running around. Then he saw a ship, whose front was shaped like a crocodile. He considered that it was a pirate ship of Croc. As he went closer he found two men in guard uniform were unconscious. He tried to wake them up, but they didn't. He took out his sword and walked forth and found two more men in guard uniform, unconscious and then he realized he had made a mistake, coming alone. He was going to return back, but then he heard a grunting sound, crying for help.

He didn't ignore and followed that voice and found a person and there were seven more men lying in guard uniforms. He lifted him and found no injury on his body, neither he was drunk but was dressed richly.

"What the hell happened here?" asked John.

"Please save my son. A pirate took him and he did something and I lost my strength."

"Who are you and why did he take your son?"

"My name is Simon and I'm the Duke of Luna. We had come for a vacation…" then he heard walking steps and a child struggling sound.

"Wait here", he suggested.

But then Simon caught his hand and asked, "at least tell me your name. I cannot see your face properly in the dark."

"My name is John Bowen from England. Please stay here. I'll get your son back. What is his name, your son?"

"Santo", answered the Duke.

He walked further leaving him in his condition. But there was something wrong; he wondered that how come they cross the Marines? Why haven't they fired any cannon, if they had to take over the city? But then he remembered that magical power of Croc. He decided to return back because he cannot fight them all alone. Then he lost his physical strength and then his consciousness and fell on the ground. Two pirates picked him and carried him inside the Ocean Jaw ship and sail away from the port along with the son of Duke.

That very night Vice Admiral Mora was reported that Duke of Luna's son and a person from England had been abducted by pirate Croc. He immediately set sail with twelve warships to the North-West which was said by a ship Captain who saw Ocean Jaw last time, when they were sailing back to Cadiz. On the way they met the English Marines with ten warships, they were hunting Morgan. Admiral Walker was also there. Mora told them that they were chasing Croc and he got John Bowen. Hearing his name Walker decided to work with Spanish fleet and rescue John and they sailed together in that direction.

* * *

Morgan and his crew arrived in one of the islands of the Azores. It was his homeland. His whole fleets of twenty-one ships were also present and they all celebrated that their Captain had broken out safely with the rest. But soon Morgan stopped the celebration because he was angry with Croc. He wanted to teach Croc a lesson that he had made mistakes. Because of him, he lost many numbers of men in which Josh his first mate was involved. He wanted to avenge them and they all were with him, but there was a problem that no one knows where Croc was or lived.

"Love, if you had something of that bastard, I could have located him", said Freya.

"Something?"

"Anything. Even a piece of his hair or a bit of his nail."

"Will this work?" he said, showing the piece of paper from the Bible, which he tore accidently when he was in Croc's cabin.

He somehow managed to keep it safe from the Marines for this time. Then Freya took the paper, rolled it round and placed it on the table in which a compass direction was drawn. She used her witchcraft powers and the rolled paper moved and rested on the point of the North-West.

"I found him, my love. He is going North-West", said Freya.

"Everyone set the sails to North-West!" ordered Morgan.

* * *

John woke up and he found himself in a cell and a huge crocodile was sleeping outside. Then he noticed there was not just one, but there were more crocodiles sleeping around. He got terrified and thought that he was the food for the crocodile and he screamed.

"Help! Help! Help!"

His noise disturbed the crocodiles and it came closer to his cage. He moved back as much as he could and the crocodiles tried to push the cage down. John again screamed for help and somebody came and the crocodiles moved back. It was a crewmate of the ship.

The person opened the cell door and said, "Come, Captain wants to see you."

The person took him to the Captain's cabin and let him enter. He saw the face of Croc. It was exactly the same face which he saw in Alma's house. He was sitting by a dining table with lots of delicious food and also the son of the Duke, Santo was sitting on one of the chairs. John felt relieved that the boy was okay.

"Hey Santo are you okay?" he asked, going to close to him.

"Yes, I'm fine and who are you?" he asked, little terrified.

"Your father sent me. Don't worry, everything will we find", he advised.

"Everything is fine, I assure you", interrupted Croc, politely. "Sit and eat as much as you want. No need to worry, no one is going to be harmed."

"Why should I trust you, the food can be poisoned?"

"Eat or starve to death. I don't have the habit of wasting food", replied Croc.

Both of them paused for a moment and watched Croc eating turkey legs piece and the delicious smell went into their nose. The boy couldn't hold his mouth watering and started eating and then John also sat on the chair and started eating as he was very hungry. After finishing the food, Croc walked out.

"Is father with you?" asked Santo.

"No, but I'll take you to him. He is fine by the way, replied John.

"And who that person?"

"Let me bother about him. And by the way, my name is John."

He and advised Santo to remain inside the cabin at all cost and he walked out on the deck. He saw the crew working without speaking any word or having any eye contact with each other, cleaning the deck and putting the sails. He looked around and saw Croc, standing on the quarterdeck.

He went to him and asked, "What is the purpose of abducting me and the boy. Asking money in exchange, I don't think it's your idea or any other pirates would prefer to do like this."

"You will know soon, Mister Bowen", said Croc.

"How do you know my name?" he asked, astonished, then he remembered about meeting his mother, "oh no need. It was your mother."

"No, it wasn't my mother and she had nothing to do with knowing your name. I just discovered it by myself when you came to see my first mate."

"First-mate?" John thought hard and remembered about Harry Smith. "...are you talking about the guy at the

Winchester? So he lied. He can be in trouble if I could get out from here."

"Don't take any foolish move, Mister Bowen. I had erased his memories and he is innocent as a usual English citizen."

"So you can erase a person's memory and that's why people don't remember your face. Are you going to kill us?"

"If I had to, I would have killed you at the harbour."

"Why are you keeping us alive and where are you taking us? What is your purpose?"

"My purpose… is to surrender."

"Surrender?" repeated John, stunned.

Croc sighed and replied, "Mister Bowen, it is your bad luck that you ended up here. My plan was to abduct the boy, but you showed up. But I had already considered that any way you will end up here, so I told the butler and my mother to tell everything if you arrive and what did you think, when strangers told you about me so easily. Even a murderer's mother tries to protect his guilty child."

John got nothing to answer. He thought he should have been aware of it.

"You know Spanish warship must be hunting you?" said John.

"Yes, I know and I wanted them to hunt me."

A storm arrived, the alliance Marine struggled to sail thought. It lasted for two nights and on the following morning they had a view of Ocean Jaw at the horizon and they followed them as fast as they could sail. After five days of the sailing, Ocean Jaw arrived at an area of the sea, which was covered with thick mist?

"Where are we?" asked John.

"Home of Ocean Jaw, where I was saved by her and I became the person you look at now", replied Croc.

John remembered a rumour about Croc and the ship.

"Wait a second I heard rumours that your ship is a living being?" he marked.

"Yes, it is. There are only four of us who are alive. You, me, the boy and the ship", he explained. "This ship is made by someone called Sobek... for the souls of the innocent people who died during the sea voyages, killed by pirates and they cannot go to the soul world. Here only, when they walk on the ship, you can touch them, physically and they act like my crewmates but they aren't and they don't speak. And as long as I'm on this ship, I have temporary powers to erase memories and make people things to do."

"What about Harry Smith?"

"I just found him, he was ship wrecked. He had a brother and he died during that time. He wanted to avenge him, so I let him to have it and I did what I should do."

"Also, according to my knowledge, you had killed some pirates?"

"Yes, I did. Because they were killed by those pirates and them- the souls were stuck in the world with vengeance."

When the mist moved away an island came forth. Ocean Jaw sailed to the island and entered through the river waterway and all the crew of Ocean Jaw disappeared into the mist. Morgan saw them sailing through the waterway but as he was thinking a strategy to surprise them, the alliance also arrived and they had a fight. They started firing the cannon on each other. Somehow, Morgan on his ship sailed away from the crossfire and Freya was with him. They went after Croc while the rest of his fleet fought the Marines. They sailed through the same waterway, into the island and soon found the Ocean Jaw ship, anchored below a water cave.

Morgan became very happy that he finally found the Ocean Jaw and ordered his men with cannons to attack, but then he didn't see any of the crew through his telescope. They anchored their ship and sailed near on small boats, armed with rifles and swords. They were also aware of the crocodiles and load their rifles and aimed to the water. Suddenly a wall came down from above and closed the Ocean Jaw inside. Morgan became very angry, but not for very long. Freya saw a boat on the bank.

Edgar kept his Bible on his court's pocket and took John and Santo to the upland and they saw two huge mountains surrounded by thick cloud.

"What is this place? Is it an island belongs to Ireland?" asked John.

"No, it isn't. I call it the Nose. It appears every ten years above the ocean", answered Croc.

"Ten years...? I didn't understand?"

"Do you look those two mountains?" he pointed.

"Seemed like two active volcanoes", marked Santo.

"No, there are not volcanoes opening, those are nostril of a creature", answered Croc.

"Nostril of a creature?" repeated John.

"What creature?" said Santo.

John still didn't understand his reference, but when he understood he was totally shocked after learning about it.

"Is the island is a living island?"

"Yes, but not exactly. We are standing on the nose of a huge creature. The mist you are watching in those mountains is what the creature is exhaling. Every ten years the creature pulls out his nose to take a breath and I consider the creature is a huge turtle believed to be alive before the dawn of time", said Croc. "Her name is Basil."

John was startled, a moment ago a living ship and ghosts and now standing on a huge turtle's nose. Back when he was at the meeting, he proved that he cannot come back to life and the Marines, who fought and killed those pirates, were nothing but Croc's copycats but believed that he had some kind of power that makes people forget his mind but this was out of his expectation. He walked a little farther away to make him convince that it was not true that he was on a giant monster's nose but neither Croc was joking. While Santo remained still, he doesn't know how to react. He was still a kid.

"This is very interesting, a giant turtle and a living ship... If I get control in both of them, then I'll be... I'll be the king... not king... I'll be the god of the seven seas", said Morgan, walking to them with thirty-seven of his crew.

"Morgan, I thought you…" said Croc little astonished.

"…Would be dead. I thought the same", he interrupted.

Croc took out a glass grenade and tossed it to them. The glass broke and emitted a large amount of green smoke and the pirates lost their physical strength and fell on the ground. He had used it back at the harbour of Cadiz. Santo ran and hid behind a tree and watched. John heard the noise and he ran back. When he reached, he found that Morgan and his men had fallen on the ground. He was also amazed that Morgan had broken out of the prison.

Freya was standing by keeping a distance. She was stunned when her party fell down under the green smoke.

"Morgan!" she said, came running.

He was near the foot of Croc.

"Help me Freya!" he replied.

"You bastard, you hurt my love. I'll not let you live peacefully for the rest of your life", said Freya and raised her hand, looked up and started to say a deadly spell.

"O dark spirits of underworld listen to your master and bring the misery, sadness and all the unhappiness to my enemies."

"Don't", warned Croc but she didn't listened.

"Go forth!" she said.

But nothing happened. It surprised her. Her deadly spell didn't work.

"My spell, it didn't work? How is this possible?" she said, while Morgan was speechless on the ground.

"You shouldn't have done that", said Croc.

Then roots came out of the ground from where Freya was standing and they caught her. Freya screamed for help and Morgan crawled to save her, but the rats consumed her into the earth.

"Give her back. Give her back. Give my Freya back", begged Morgan, sobbing.

He turned to Croc and crawled back to him.

"It's because of you, it's because of you, my Freya is gone", he blamed him. "Give her back, give her back."

"I can't, the creature prohibits witches or any other evil sorcery", answered Croc.

The Spanish and the English Marine ships arrived, only three of their ship was destroyed by the cannon crossfire, but Morgan's fleets were completely destroyed and those who survived the crossfire were arrested. They arrived by the same water pass and took down the last ship of Morgan. Then they found John and the rest.

Morgan and Croc were arrested including the remaining of Morgan's crew and were brought to England. Santo was taken to his parents and John also returned to England. All the credits were given to John for catching the two pirate Captains and trying to save the son of a Duke Simon. John became a hero and he got the bounty money, which was on Croc and Morgan. After three days, the pirates were held for the court trial and were convicted guilty and executed on the same day. John retired from the Marines as he had told his wife and invested the bounty money in the hotel business. It went well, but not as he expected. He needed a business partner who could support his business and he found one. He was a Spanish merchant, living in England with his mother. His named was Edgar Leonor.

- **Charles E. Ekka**

3. The Missing Crown

After travelling to several friendly residents, Luke returned to his palace. He was the King of Aspaca. He looked old now but he had more wisdom and strength than before. He had a beautiful and kind daughter, named Rebecca. She had a curious mind to know about things that catch her attention. He was sixteen years old when he first stepped into the battlefield after his older brother got killed and his father was left injured by foe's arrow. The invaders were vast but Luke created a new battle tactic against them and led his whole army to victory. For that courageous act, he was praised by his people of his kingdom.

He was with his twenty-five finest Royal guards, guarding his Royal carriage and was led by Commander Thomas who was a loyal and devoted man to his King and to his duty. He respected him more than any other since he first met and fought alongside in the battlefield. The Royal carriage stopped near the palace's main entrance and the servants nearby bowed in respect. A foot guard opened the carriage's door and Luke walked out, holding a book. Thomas joined him while the rest took Thomas's horse and the carriage to the stable. They passed the Royal hall and walked up the stairs to the first floor. A maid was walking down, holding empty silver dishes, when she noticed the King and the Commander, coming to her way. She stopped and bowed to them. When Luke passed by her, he noticed that she was his daughter's chambermaid. He stopped by her.

"How is my daughter?" he asked.

"Your Majesty, she has almost recovered from her fever, and a while ago she ate her meal and went to sleep", replied the maid, humbly.

"Okay, let her sleep", he replied and walked to his chamber.

Two guards were guarding his chamber door and the guard standing on the right side opened it. They entered and Luke placed the book on his bookshelf and took off his crown and placed it on the table, next to his bed. He removed his court by himself and dropped it on the ground.

"Your Majesty, are you going to have dinner?" asked Thomas.

"No Thomas, my stomach is full and I'm very tired. I need some rest", he replied.

"As your wish... Good night, Your Majesty. I'll serve you in the morning", said Thomas and walked out of the chamber.

Luke changed his clothes into pyjama and fetched himself a glass of wine from the jug kept on his writing table. He drank it and went to sleep. Next morning Luke woke up early and felt very refreshing. He was completely healed from yesterday's tiredness. He yawned and stretched his arms. He gazed to the window and then turned to get off the bed. As his feet touched the ground, he noticed something was missing and then he was shocked. It was his crown, missing from its place. He stood up and looked around his chamber. The crown was nowhere to be seen.

"Guards! Guards!" cried Luke and the two guards standing outside, rushed inside.

One of them asked, "Your Majesty, what happened?"

"My crown, my crown is missing", he replied. "Somebody had stolen it. Summon Commander Thomas now!"

The same guard ran out, while other stayed with the King and he alerted everyone by ranging the King's bell. It was outside and near the King's chamber and it alerted the guards present at different places, inside the palace boundary. The palace main gate was closed and the sound was even heard by few citizens of city Lear which was close to the palace.

Thomas arrived immediately. Luke told him about the stolen crown and he was shocked. He promised the King that he will find the crown and the thief. He investigated and learnt by the King's two night guards that they allowed three maids to enter the King's chamber when he was asleep, to pick his travelling dirty clothes for washing. They were the regular maids who only work and clean the King's chamber, that's why they allowed them to enter and then in the morning the crown went missing and if someone had tried to take away the crown through the window then the night guards outside would have seen the thief, easily. And so the three maids were convicted guilty and were imprisoned, even though they sobbed and strongly denied of stealing the crown and the two-night guards were also imprisoned for failing to guard the King's door.

Thomas and some other guards went and searched the chamber of the three maids but the crown wasn't there and that led Thomas to suspect if more of the Royal servants were involved in the theft. And so, all the Royal servant's chambers were searched and still then the crown was nowhere to be found. Then Thomas discussed something with Luke and summoned all the Royal servants in the throne chamber and they were surrounded by the Royal guards in case if anyone tried to escape. Till then the news of the stolen crown, somehow made way through the palace boundary and reached to city Lear and was still spreading beyond.

Princess Rebecca also arrived and stood by her father. He was sitting on his throne chair and was very angry. When she first heard about the theft from her chambermaid, she first thought to catch the thief and punish him for the crime but when she heard about the three maids who work in her father's chamber, her thoughts changed.

"Why the three maids would do that type of crime? They knew clearly that the punishment for stealing a Royal property is death?" What were they trying to gain? And why didn't they ran away?" she questioned to herself.

"Listen..." spoke Thomas, gently to the Royal servants. "Till now you all have known that Our Majesty's crown is stolen and who has stolen it. But we haven't found the crown yet and I suspect that other than the three maids more people are involved in the theft. And I demand the crown thief if he or she is among you, surrender now with the crown and the person will not be charged death penalty."

All the servants murmured among each other.

"I didn't steal the crown. I was in my chamber when this incident happened." "I was there too; I mean I was sleeping in my chamber." "Who could have stolen it?" "They suspect one of us is a thief." "I'm not the thief." "Me neither." "Help me, God. I'm not the thief."

Meanwhile, Rebecca thought who could have stolen the crown and one thing she was sure that her chambermaid, Mary couldn't be involved in theft, neither all the other servants but only one or maybe two or three must be involved? And at some point, her thought was that the three maids who were imprisoned were innocent.

"Come forth and surrender and this is my last warning!" said Thomas and the servants got scared and became silent and nobody came forward, all remained facing down.

"Threatening the Royal servants won't be helpful in achieving the stolen crown or the thief, Sir Thomas", interrupted Rebecca and walked forward to defend the servants.

"Rebecca", said Luke, from his throne chair.

"Pardon me, Princess, it's my job to catch the thief and bring him to King's justice", replied Thomas, politely.

"Rebecca! It is not your job", exclaimed the King.

"But father, have you thought what any of the Royal servants would have gained in stealing the Royal crown", explained Rebecca, quickly.

But the King didn't listen. He became very angry but then Thomas interrupted.

"Pardon me Your Majesty, but I think you should let the Princess to speak. Let us listen to her to what she has to say", suggested Thomas.

He looked to Rebecca, still angry but he permitted.

"Thank you father", she replied. She continued to explain, "father the three maids whom you imprisoned have served us for over decades and if they were or they are the thieves, then they would have known clearly that punishment for stealing a Royal property is execution and risk to steal only the crown is a stupid idea."

"What are trying to say?" asked the King.

"There are many silver dishes which can easily be stolen from the Royal kitchen and why didn't they steal them? And why didn't they run away after stealing the crown?"

"You have a good point, Princess", said Thomas. "But we shouldn't forget that they were the only people, who entered the King's chamber before the crown went missing. And the crown cannot move on its own but can be moved by a person and... that is a thief could do that and they are the three maids."

"But what if they are innocent?" added the Princess.

"Then who is the thief? Who stole the crown?" questioned Thomas. "And I suspect that one or may be two thieves are among them. And I will take all the necessary steps to find him and when they all were caught, and then we will ask them that why didn't they runway?"

Rebecca got nothing to reply. There was a silent for a second. Thomas turned to the Royal servants and said the warning again, yet no one came forward.

"Fine then", said Thomas.

He called a guard and talked with him in silent to deal with the three maids and the Royal servants whom he thinks might be involved in theft.

"I think I know something about the crown!" interrupted a servant.

Her statement shocked everyone and they turned to her. Rebecca was more shocked because it was Mary, her chambermaid.

"W-what did you say?" asked Luke.

"Your Majesty, I think I know something about the crown", said Mary, little terrified.

"You mean you know who could have stolen the crown", marked Thomas.

"No, I don't", she replied and turned to the King, "Your Majesty, yesterday evening, when I was taking the dishes to the kitchen, I encountered you and Sir Thomas. That moment I noticed that you.... You were not having the crown on your head."

Her statement startled everyone. The servants murmured among themselves.

"She didn't saw the crown?" "But the crown was stolen from the King's chamber, right?" "I don't know who stole the crown but I'm not the one." "Me neither." "She didn't saw the crown then where is the crown?"

"Silence!" said one of the guards, surrounded them.

"You know what you are saying?" asked Thomas.

"Yes, I know and I told you, what I saw", she replied.

Thomas thought that she must be lying and she must also be involved in theft, but then an old maid named Martha came forward and claimed that when the King walked out of the carriage, she also didn't saw the crown. Everyone was puzzled but not Thomas. He considered that Mary and Martha were both involved in theft and now they were trying to distract the real issue.

"Liars", declared Thomas. "Stop lying."

"I'm not lying", claimed Mary.

"Me neither", said Martha.

Rebecca quickly turned to her father and said, "father, are you sure that you have the crown with you?"

Luke grunted and then replied, "O-Of... course", he was not sure.

"Your Majesty, can I have your command to arrest these liars?" asked Thomas. "I think when they will be tortured, and then only they will stop speaking lies and speak the truth."

"Please don't interrupted, Sir Thomas", said Rebecca. "My father is trying to remember it."

"But Your Majesty had answered that he remembered and I was there too, I remember too."

"Are you sure?"

"Of..."

"Silence, you two!" said Luke and they became silent.

They both apologised and there was silent for a moment. Luke again asked the two maids that are they sure because he too couldn't remember the crown and they both replied yes. Then two guards entered the throne chamber and they were the guards who were with the King during the journey and one of them said, "Excuse us My Lord and sorry to interrupt. We both request to speak something."

"What is it?" asked Luke.

"Your Majesty, it is about the crown", he said

"Yes, I'm listening."

"We heard the conversation from outside that two of them claimed that they didn't see the crown and we both also didn't see the crown, when we returned from the journey and we also discussed about it while taking the horses to the stable and we considered that you must be holding it and we didn't notice."

"Yes, Your Majesty, I was with him", said the other guard.

Everybody kept thinking. It was very puzzling and two servants murmured among themselves. "What, the guards didn't see the crown, the maids didn't see the crown...?" "What is going on?"

"Silence! Who told you to talk?" said a guard and then one of them spoke, "Why are we suspected? The guards could be involved in the theft?"

"Yes, you are right", said another servant.

"Silence!" said the same guard again.

"I think you are involved in theft and trying to blame us", said a servant.

The guard got scared, but he replied grunting, "Aaa... I... I will not do the crime. I have taken the oath to serve the King."

"So I... and other servants have", he turned to Luke and said, "Your Majesty, we love and respect you with all our heart and we wouldn't have done that kind of crime to hurt you or to hurt ourselves."

"Father, it seemed like your crown was never been stolen from your chamber at all, maybe you left somewhere else during the travel", concluded Rebecca, thoughtfully, "and you might have forgotten it."

The King thought about yesterday till going to bed. He took a long moment and then he answered, "I don't know. I'm confused. I can only remember the weight of the crown on my head."

Rebecca went close to him and requested, "father please try to remember or the innocent will be killed."

"I cannot remember the crown. I remember the fun and the taste of food and wine and after this I'm confused", he replied.

He was not the only one, everyone was confused, even Thomas. Where the crown flew? Thomas tried to remember about yesterday morning till evening but he now too couldn't remember seeing the crown. He could have blamed the two guards that they are liars, but he didn't because he knew them well and he was the one who selected them to be the guard for the King's journey and if he did, then all will be suspected and could lead to nowhere.

Then Rebecca decided that she will travel back to all the residents where her father had visited yesterday and look for the crown. After thinking for a moment and considering that she was now well from fever the King permitted and commanded Thomas to go with her. And it was decided that till then the three maids will be in prison and if she fails to find the crown, the three maids will be tortured and will be questioned about the crown and then they will be executed. Thomas summoned the same number of men who was with the King yesterday and they soon set on the journey.

The first destination was the Saint Benjamin's Church in the middle of city Lear. The King had arrived yesterday for Sunday morning mass. Rebecca arrived in her Royal carriage with her guards and came off the carriage. The church door was open and the priest was cleaning the dust with a broom. He saw the Princess and the Royal guards entering. He stopped working.

"Pardon me Princess; I have to clean the house of God. Then you can pray", he said, politely.

"Forgive me Father to interrupt, but we are in hurry and we have to ask something very quick", replied Rebecca.

"What is it child?" he asked.

"Father, yesterday morning my father came for the morning mass, did he mistakenly leave his crown in the church?" she answered.

The priest thought and replied, "No he didn't. If he had left it, I would have noticed it first and would have returned it to the right hands. Anyway let me ask someone else too."

He turned and called an altar boy named Ford. He was cleaning the room behind the altar when he heard his name called out. The priest asked him about the crown and he replied the same and also told that when the King left the church, the crown was with him.

"Thank you father, for your time", said Rebecca and the priest nodded once.

The next resident was the house of a rich merchant. He was the richest person in the city of Lear, where Luke went to talk about the trading business. Rebecca asked him about the crown and he answered the same as the priest. Then they went to an Earl's house. His name was Robert and lived near a coastal town and it took more than three hours to reach there. Yesterday at his house including the King, they celebrated the forty-ninth birth of Robert by singing, eating, drinking and dancing.

When Princess and her guards arrived, Robert gave her a warm welcome by standing outside the door as if he knew that she would come. She greeted "good afternoon", to him and they walked inside the house.

"Princess, I heard you were sick, yesterday", said Robert.

"Yes, and I'm better now."

"Is that true your father's crown was stolen?"

"Yes, but how did you know?"

"I heard from one of my servants and he heard from a person from the market. News from the Nobles spread quicker than you ride, isn't it?"

Then she told him about the purpose of her visit.

"No Princess, your father didn't leave his crown. If had, I would have sent someone to deliver it, immediately."

"When my father left your house, did you saw having it?"

"Hmm... I was drunk but yes I remember that he was having it."

"Anyway thank you for giving me your time", she greeted with a slight bow.

"Anytime", he replied, as she was going to leave, "Princess... my wife wants to speak with you", he interrupted.

Her name was Elizabeth, she requested Rebecca to join them for lunch. Rebecca couldn't refuse as she was also hungry and her guards were also given meal to eat and drink but not wine.

"Princess, can I ask you something?" said Elizabeth.

"Yes, what is it?" she replied.

"Why are you talking so much trouble to search the crown if it is left somewhere?"

"What you mean?"

"My wife means that you could have sent a rider to us to ask about it", explained Elizabeth.

"I thought the same at first but later I decided, it would better that I should go by myself and search it", replied Rebecca. "We suspect... I mean the Lord Commander Thomas suspect that one of the thieves is among the servant and then it is suspected that the thief is among everyone inside the palace and so we sent no rider."

"Nice decision", said Elizabeth. "Did you come up with?"

"Yes."

"And what do you think who is the thief?" asked Robert.

"I'm not sure. I don't think it was stolen. My father might have left his crown somewhere else and forgot."

"And what if the crown was not found like you think. I guess there no other place to go?"

"Yes there is one."

"Okay and what if you don't find it there?"

"We will think later."

After finishing the lunch and before parting, Robert suggested the Princess that he suspects that it was stolen and not forgotten. Then they returned to Lear and went to a bookstore which was the largest bookstore in the city.

"Why my father came to a bookstore?" asked Rebecca to Thomas. "He could have sent someone else."

"I asked the same but your father said that he just wants to get the book by himself", answered Thomas.

Rebecca asked the lady owner about the crown.

"Crown? But I heard sometimes ago that the thieves are caught. Didn't they?"

"No, it's not like that... we believe my father may have left mistakenly in your bookstore, now can you tell me did my father left his crown here?"

"Forgive me, Princess", said the owner, bowing.

"Franklin! Franklin!" she cried.

"Yes! What is it?" he replied coming and then bowed as he saw the gorgeous Princess. He was a handsome young boy and Princess fell in love at first sight.

"Franklin, Princess wants to know if her father had left his crown in the bookstore?" said the owner.

"No, my Lady, Majesty came yesterday, took his book and returned", he replied politely.

"And did you see the crown on his head?" asked Thomas interrupting and Rebecca was surprised.

The boy thought for a moment. "The far I can remember, I saw the crown on his head", he answered.

"Are you sure?"

"Yes sir, I'm."

Thomas sighed, "Okay." And he walked out.

"Okay Franklin, you can get on your work", said the lady owner and turned to the Princess. "Your Grace, I'm sorry we couldn't help you and if we had the crown, we would have returned it."

"That's okay", replied the Princess. "Pardon me", said the lady owner and went on her work.

Rebecca also turned to go but the boy said, "Excuse me, Princess."

She swiftly turned to him and said, "Yes."

"Can I know your name?" he asked swiftly and sounded absurdly and then he realized quickly and said, "My humble apologies for speaking absurdly, I just rushed all of a sudden. Sorry", he said, bowing.

"That's wasn't absurd", she replied. "My name is Rebecca", and he rose straight.

"Princess Rebecca, it's been an honour to meet you in person", he replied. "It is true that you are beautiful like shinning stars like I heard."

"Princess we need to return", called Thomas.

"Pardon me, I have to go", she said to the boy and she turned.

"Franklin", said the boy. "My name is Franklin."

She turned and smiled to him. "I know", she replied and walked out of the bookstore and sat in her Royal carriage.

Franklin followed her outside and watched her carriage leaving and he smiled.

"We will meet again Princess, very soon", he commented.

Rebecca was smiling and thinking about him and then she remembered that she hadn't found the crown and that made her upset. They returned back to the palace and when they arrived at the main entrance, Thomas became angry to see the three maids and the two-night guards who were supposed to be in prison, were standing outside. Princess walked out of her carriage and she was surprised to see them. Thomas asked the foot guards that who allowed them to go free? He was sure that they were the thieves since they didn't found the crown but one of the foot guard replied that the King had bailed them for not committing the crime and the crown was found.

Thomas and Rebecca were shocked, including the guards who went with them. The three maids were waiting for the Princess to thank her because they heard that she tried to defend her and Rebecca said sorry to them because she failed to defend them. It was a coincidence that the crown was found.

"When the crown did was found?" asked Thomas.

"I think in the mid noon and Your Majesty has told you both to meet him in his chamber as soon as you arrive", replied the foot guard.

Rebecca and Thomas went immediately to the King's chamber and wondered with a lot of question like, who was the crown thief and did he surrender himself? How did he steal the crown, when there was no escape? They knocked the door and Luke permitted to come inside. They both looked around the chamber but they didn't saw the crown.

"Father the foot guard told that you have found the crown", said Rebecca.

"Yes, it is found", he replied.

"Who was the thief?" asked Thomas.

"Where is the crown?" asked Rebecca.

"No one had stolen it", answered the King. "And it is right there?" showing the table where he always kept his crown before sleeping. They both felt awkward because there was nothing on the table. "Go and see for yourself", to his daughter.

She walked close and looked over the table. She couldn't understand what his father was trying to show. She thought that the table had a secret drawer and she moved her right palm over it and as her palm was few inches away from the table surface, she felt something pointy and quickly moved back her hand.

"What happened, Princess?" asked Thomas.

"I felt something", she replied.

"The thing you felt is my crown", explained Luke, "it has become invisible and it was right there for the whole time."

They both were stunned. Then Thomas moved and picked the crown and he was speechless. He felt the presence but cannot see. He placed it back on the table.

"How did you discover it?" asked the Princess.

The King explained that when they left to search for the crown, he came to his chamber and thought a lot that why the three maids stole the crown? And why the other maids didn't see the crown? Accidently he placed his palm on the table and quickly moved back when he felt something. At first, he got scared, what was that nail like thing? When he touched slowly, he felt it again. It was round and it was familiar. He covered it with a small cloth and it appeared in the shape of the crown. He also showed some of the guards and they were also shocked and terrified.

"Oh God, I almost killed the innocent", said Thomas.

"Is it some kind of magic?" asked Rebecca, astonishingly.

"Yes, indeed", declared Thomas.

"Who could have done this?"

"Right now, I have no name in my mind", said Thomas.

"Neither I, it could be anybody. And we shouldn't take any reckless action like before, we should be more careful", suggested the King.

"So what shall we do now?" said the Princess. "Do we know someone who can help us?"

"I have sent my messenger to bring the priest; he would be arriving at any moment", replied Luke. "I think he might know something about this."

"Hope he should", said Thomas.

At the same moment, a guard knocked the chamber's door and informed that the priest had arrived. Luke permitted to let him through. He was the same person whom Rebecca met at the church. His name was Father Carlos.

"You remembered me, Your Majesty", said Carlos.

"Yes, father", replied Luke. "I need your help."

The King told him about the invisible crown. First, he didn't believe it but when the priest moved his hand and touched the invisible crown, he was stunned and scared and moved back.

"What was that unholy thing", he said, holding his cross.

And that scared the other people inside the chamber for a moment and he kept on gazing the table.

"Father, are you okay?" asked Thomas.

"No, I'm not", he replied, scared.

"What is it, father? Why the crown has become invisible?" asked Rebecca.

"I think... it is some kind of witchcraft related that has made it invisible", he replied.

"Witchcraft, I was just having the same though", said Luke.

"How did this happen?" asked Carlos to Thomas.

"We don't know, we just arrived and learnt about it, just before you arrived", answered Thomas.

"Can you pray and remove the evil enchantment and make it visible again?" asked the King.

The priest was still scared but he gained his courage by his faith. He looked at him and said, "Yes."

The priest prayed and poured Holy water over the crown. The crown was visible again for a second and became invisible. After trying several times the priest gave up. He said that the witchcraft had taken over the crown completely and suggested that it was better to get rid of it.

"Isn't there any other thing that can be done? Or is there any person who can help us?" asked Thomas to the priest.

The priest thought. "Well... I think there is a person who can help. I had met him a long time ago", he replied.

"Who is that person you are talking about?" asked Thomas.

"His name is Gefion? He is an outcaste, live somewhere in the forest which is on the eastern outskirts of the Kingdom. I cannot describe how he looks but I think he could tell you what you are dealing with and who had done that enchantment?" said the priest.

"Gefion? Sounds like I have heard from someone's tongue. Wait, I had heard rumours of him. Is that kind of person really exists", replied Thomas. The priest nodded. "Who is this person?"

"Don't have a word to define his profession but yes, he exists or could be dead by now, that I'm not sure but he is the one who can help us know about this", answered the priest.

The priest returned back and Luke ordered Thomas to find him and bring him and declared that he will be awarded one hundred gold coins if he successfully able to remove the invisible curse and hunt down the person who did it?

Thomas set with twenty riders to find that person who might or might not be dead. They asked the shepherds and some travellers and the local villagers. Many of them said that they don't knew or heard of a person of that name and some claimed of seeing him but no one knew where he lived. Some said he might live in this village and some said he might live in that village but he was neither on that village.

After thirty days of search, Thomas finally found him. He brought him to the palace and introduced him to the King and the Princess. He was an old man, looked over hundred years old but walk like a youth and got his own splendid horse. Thomas doubted first when he claimed to be Gefion and they met him near the river stream when he was also fetching water to his horse. But when the old man took the name of all the twenty riders, they all were amazed. Then he said the name of the places they travelled to search him and described about the people who claimed to know him whom Thomas and his men met during the search. He proved that he was not an ordinary person. He had the ability to read people's mind. They took him to the King's chamber and showed him.

"Can I have your permission to hold it, Your Majesty", asked the old man and he allowed.

He picked it up and wasn't surprised. "Hmm... well so it's really invisible", he said.

"Is it witchcraft doing this to the crown?" asked Rebecca.

"Yes, indeed", he answered, nodding.

"Can you explain something about this?" asked Thomas.

"I would also like to know about it", said Luke.

"This is rare but still very dangerous", explained Gefion, placed the crown back on the table and turned to them. "I have only seen twice in my entire life in other countries and the first time in this condition. In both the cases the witches make children invisible completely and I mean like a spirit that cannot be touched, heard or felt and leave their parents or loved ones searching for life. It is kind of blackmail to the children's parents and instead something kind of particular thing was demanded from the parents and in return to see the children again."

"Did you able to help those children?" asked Rebecca.

"Yes and as for this invisible crown, the spell is incomplete, I can undo it easily", said Gefion.

"So do it? Or you need something else?" asked Thomas.

"Yes, first I would like to see my payment that I was promised", he demanded.

Luke took out a purse from his pocket and showed him. "I'm holding it, in my hand", he said.

"Okay, then and now I only need a fireplace or just a fire container will be enough."

They walked out, holding the invisible crown, wrapped in a cloth and went near a fire container, which was used to light the palace during night. One of the foot guards placed lumber in the container and set the fire. Then Gefion took out a small bottle of salt like thing and poured into the fire. The salt cracked and emitted blue smoke and he took the crown from the King and lifted it into the smoke. After few seconds the crown was visible again. Everyone present near him was stunned. He handed back the crown to Luke and he was very happy seeing it. Luke gave him his full payment and he was happy with it. Now there was still one work left. The four of them went to the meeting hall.

"So who could be the witch?" asked Luke.

"It is strange that why the witch didn't use full power spell to make the crown invisible completely and according to my knowledge the Princess should be the target? Your Majesty, when did you last saw your crown visible?" said Gefion.

"I don't know clearly, I just felt that I was having the crown on my head and reacted like usual", replied Luke.

"Even I felt like, Your Majesty was having the crown", said Thomas.

"And got any demanding threats from someone? It actually happened in my previous incidents."

"No, not at all", answered the King, simply.

"Okay then, what exactly happened that day, when the crown became invisible? What were you doing?"

The King told him about visiting several friendly residents till going to bed and the wrongly accusing his chambermaids and the guards who claimed not seeing the crown. Then the Princess told her part and where everyone claimed that they saw the King having the crown.

"I think I know who the witch is?" considered Gefion.

"Who is it? Was she among the Royal servants?" asked Thomas, curiously.

"And one more thing I want to know", said Gefion.

"What?"

"Did something else happen till now, something strange events that were not normal to your surroundings, during the time when you were searching for me?"

The King and the Princess thought and said that nothing had happened strange during that time.

"If that so, the person is from outside and there is no denying, no one is from inside the palace", declared Gefion.

"How can say that?" asked Thomas.

Gefion explained like that said that the two maids and two guards claimed that they didn't see the crown when the King entered the palace and according to Rebecca the bookstore was the last destination where people saw the crown visible which means the witch they were hunting, must be from that bookstore and if the witch was among the people inside the palace, she won't be sitting quite till now.

"Then we must immediately arrest her", said Thomas.

"I think it must be the lady owner", considered Rebecca.

"I will ban that store. Don't know, what more trouble she will cause", said Luke. "Or she is doing it for a long time."

Something struck on Gefion's mind and he said, "Did you mention that you bought a book?"

"Yes", replied the King.

"Can I see it?"

"But why? What is so important?"

"I can only say if I see that book by myself."

They went back to the King's chamber. Luke searched the book from the bookshelf and found it and he hadn't opened it since then. The title was 'History of Rome'. It was a thick book with green cover. He handed it to Gefion and he shuffled the pages. While shuffling, he found a brown card.

"Alas, my expectation was true", said Gefion, picking the card.

"What is that?" asked Luke. "Wait, I think I remember. It is the page marker."

"No, this isn't a page marker", answered Gefion. "A spell is written on it. And you must have read it."

Luke thought and he remembered that he may have read it.

"Yes, I think so", he said.

"Is it the spell that made the crown invisible?" asked Rebecca.

"Yes and now I understand that why the spell was weak? The witch didn't read the spell but Your Majesty did. The witch was around when the spell was read", explained Gefion.

Luke became very angry and he commanded Thomas to arrest her immediately. Gefion burned that card on the fire container and then him, Thomas and along with ten guards; they rode to that bookstore. They raided that place and searched for something like animal body parts or bones or anything strange that shouldn't be in the bookstore. Gefion read the mind of the lady owner and three of her employees and they came out clean, neither Thomas nor his guards found anything related to witchcraft. Thomas thought for a moment that Gefion consideration was false but then they learnt that one of the employs was on leave and his name was Franklin.

They got his address from the lady owner and rode to his house. He was not at home. The landlord of the house was shocked that his customer was a criminal because he was very nice with him. They didn't mention him to be a witch but a burglar so that the words won't spread and the civilians may not panic and kill each other in fear. They also checked his room where he rests and found nothing except for a bed with a pillow.

"Where is he?" asked Thomas to the landlord.

"I don't know sir, he said he will be back after five days and that was two days since he left", answered the landlord.

"Are you trying to hide him?"

"No, no I'm not. I will kill him for whatever crime he has done."

They also raided the landlord's house and didn't find any evidence of the witch. Thomas decided and ordered four of his men to patrol around that area. They hadn't seen his face except for him and the landlord. So he asked the landlord to inform his men when he shows up. The landlord agreed but then as Gefion was going to read his mind he remembered.

"Sir, I think I know where he may have gone", he claimed coming close to them.

"Where?" asked Thomas.

"There a farmhouse at the outskirts of the city and he once took me... and... he was there for five days once and then came back to work in the city and live in my house", he answered.

Thomas and Gefion talked and decided to check out the farmhouse. The landlord led them and reached to a hilly region and down the slope; there was the house with empty animal shelters. The landlord stayed with two guards and watched the horses and the rest went down the slope. They were not sure if he was in the house or not but they took precaution and went close by hiding behind trees. Suddenly, Franklin came out holding an axe. Thomas was almost seen but he was not noticed. He chopped some logs and got inside.

As he went inside the house, they sneaked towards the door and took out their swords. Then they charged into the house and caught him empty handed, practising witchcraft. It was him and had made a circle and star in it and on the each point of the star; he had kept fresh chopped head of sheep and pigs. He was burning the lumbers at the fireplace when they changed in and took him by surprise. His house was stinking with rotten smell and he had hanged the bodies and head of other farm animals.

Gefion found a book which was about witchcraft cult and a sketch of a girl on the table. When Thomas saw the sketch, he was stunned because it was the face of Rebecca.

"We found the witch", declared Gefion.

"He will feel sorry for it", commented Thomas.

They brought him to the palace and question him in the prison. He didn't speak at first but after lashing him several times, he admitted that he accidently placed the magic spell card in between the pages of the book that the King took. He was preparing to get it back by enchanting the Princess thought her dream and he was preparing it for last thirty days.

Luke and Thomas were relieved that they caught him in at the right moment. Franklin was trial where he was found guilty immediately with evidence that he was a witch and then he was burnt alive in front of the crowd. His landlord, the priest, Lord Robert and the rich merchant and the Lady owner was also present there. Rebecca became very upset but she moved on. Finally, Gefion climbed on his horse and returned to the wilderness.

- **Charles E. Ekka**

4. The Wilkinson's Haunting

Joyce Wilkinson was sleeping with her six years old daughter, Alicia, when she felt very warm on her face. She woke up and was stunned. Her room was on fire. She grabbed her daughter and immediately ran out of the room. Kevin, their old butler was coming to help them and he found them on the hallway. They all immediately ran out of the house including the other four servants. None of them was hurt but the house didn't.

Next morning, Joyce's husband Martin Wilkinson returned by morning train. He was a wealthy man and owned a gun manufacturing company from his birth right and also loved horse riding. It was passed from his grandfather Lawrence, who also raised him when he lost his parents. His father died when he accidentally shot himself while cleaning a handgun and his mother died of cancer. He had gone to London for a business trip and it went great. He was returning happily and had brought gifts for her daughter and wife. But when he arrived to his house, he was shocked seeing the scenario. Joyce, Kevin along with eight police men were waiting for him. Martin went and hugged his wife.

"Martin... our house is no more", she said, sorrowfully.

"How this happened? And where is Alicia?" he replied, frustrated.

"Everyone is safe, sir. No one is hurt", interrupted Kevin.

"Kevin, how did this happen? And why didn't you write a letter to inform me?" asked Martin to Kevin.

"It happened last night", answered Kevin.

"Yes Martin, it happened last night", said Joyce.

Martin looked to his house. The left side portion was burnt and collapsed and little of the right portion of the house was left. He felt very sad about the house because it was his family house and he was brought by playing around.

One of the policemen was Inspector Turner, who was given in charge to investigate the cause of the fire. He called Martin and questioned him in private, if there was anyone who wants to kill them? Or got any death threats? Or he had any argument with any random stranger? Martin thought hard and answered that he had no enemies or got any death threats but he agreed that he had an argument with a random stranger but it was very long time ago and he doesn't remember his face or the cause of the argument.

"Okay Mr. Wilkinson, if you remember anything else, report me while I and my team will investigate the cause of the fire", said Turner.

"How did this happen?" asked Martin.

"I told you, we are investigating and we will report you if we find anything."

"How long will it take?"

"Cannot promise but it shouldn't take very long."

Then the Wilkinsons and their butler returned to the hotel where they were living after the incident including their servants. There were two local reporters waiting for them at the hotel lobby. They rushed to ask questions when they saw them coming but Kevin blocked them.

"Mr. Wilkinson, Mrs. Wilkinson, how did your house burnt?"

"Mr. Wilkinson, is someone injured?"

"Everyone is safe and sound and we don't know the cause of fire... leave my master alone, come back later. He is very tired now", declared Kevin.

Later while having dinner, Martin ate nothing. He kept on thinking about something and when asked by Joyce, he replied that he was thinking how the house burnt? He then became angry by over thinking and hammered the dining table with his fist.

"Damn it", he said.

Alicia got scared and she was about to sob. Joyce scolded Martin and he realized his mistake and apologized to Alicia. His anger cooled down and realized that his family was still with him and it's his responsibility to protect them at any cost. Later, Joyce suggested him that he should look for a new house and Martin agreed. After a while, Kevin arrived with new clothes for them. He had gone to buy with Daisy and Emily- the house maids. Next day the reporters arrived again to the hotel and this time Joyce and Martin gave their statements that police were investigating the cause of fire and no one was hurt during the incident. One of the reporter asked if it was done by an outside person and Martin replied that he had no enemies who would kill him. Then Martin went to his gun manufacturing factory, where some of his employees were glad that his family was okay.

"Thank you everyone for carrying, everything is fine, get back to work", he replied.

In the evening, when he returned, he found that her daughter was unwrapping something. It was one of the gifts which he had bought for his wife from London. It was a lady's purse, a very expensive one. After that, he remembered the gift for her daughter and took out the briefcase, which he had not opened since yesterday he arrived from London. He took out the gift and gave it to her. It was a stuff girl doll.

"Did you like it?" he asked, smiling.

"Yes yes, I loved it", replied Alicia, nodding.

"Say thank you to your papa", said Joyce.

"Thank you, papa", she said.

"Why thank you, I'm her father. She doesn't need to? It's my duty to keep her happy."

"Come on Martin, she needs to learn some good manners", and he got nothing to reply.

He picked the purse and gave it to Joyce.

"This was for you", he said, smiling.

Joyce didn't like it but she accepted his gift. After a while, they had a knock at the door. It was a police constable and he told that they had recovered some of their belongings that had survived the fire and to recover them, they need to come to the police station. Martin went with Kevin and after an hour they returned, holding the staffs. They had brought two undamaged portraits, a vase, some spoons, and three hats, a two pair of boots, some Joyce's jewellery and some books.

"Did the inspector told about the cause of the fire?" asked Joyce.

"No, he didn't. He is still investigating."

"And what about our new house?" remarked Joyce.

"I had told my manager, he will look for it", he said to Joyce. "And Kevin did I told you to informed our lawyer."

"Yes sir, I have informed him."

They kept all the staff on the table and went to have dinner. Next morning their family lawyer came and handed them their new copy of property papers.

"That was very quick", marked Joyce, thinking it would have taken many days.

"That's because, I don't mix, all the property files, Mrs. Wilkinson", replied the lawyer.

Martin checked all the papers while Joyce looked the stuff which had survived the fire. She checked her hats and found that one of it had a burnt hole in it. She felt little upset because it was her favourite hat. Then she looked her jewellery. All pieces were there and had slightly melted. She kept it in her new purse and then she checked the books, which were still in good condition. But then she found that one of them was not a book; it was a photo album which she had never seen before. She recognized her young husband and his parents and her grandfather-in-law- Lawrence and his wife in the photos and there were many new faces during the time of young Lawrence.

Then Martin signed those papers and the lawyer's work was done and he was gone. Joyce showed Martin the photo album and asked him if he remembers about this photo album and he was surprised. It was the first time he was also seeing it. He recognized almost all the people. They were his parent's relatives, cousins of his parents and grandparents and their friends but he hadn't seen those photos or the album. They thought Kevin might know about this and they went to his room and asked him. He thought for a while and he remembered about it.

"Oh, I remember. It was Master Lawrence's personal photo album which he always kept with himself and only once or twice I had seen it on his hand", he replied, looking through the photos.

In one family photo, little young Lawrence and his grandfather and the whole family with servants were standing in front of the house and in another photo, old Lawrence with his wife, little young Martin and his parents with all the present servants were there. Joyce smiled seeing her young husband; he was fat.

"And sir, what about the house, are you going to rebuild it?" asked Kevin.

"Haven't decided yet", he answered. "But, I may rebuild it."

Joyce looked both the photo of a different generation of Wilkinsons and thought about the day when she first met Martin at Cambridge University. Suddenly, she noticed something difference between the photos of young Martin and young Lawrence family photo. The house in the background was not the same. In young Martin's family photo house was the house, where they stayed and it was now burnt down and in young Lawrence's family photo house was completely different one. She showed it to her husband.

"Oh, you are right", he replied, amazed.

Then Kevin looked and said, "I think, it must be that old house of your grandfather. He lived when he was very young."

"Old house? Never heard that my family own another house?" questioned Martin.

"What you don't know about it?" replied Kevin. "I thought you knew about..."

"No, I haven't."

"Oh my apologies", said Kevin.

He understood that why Martin didn't know about the old house because Lawrence died before telling him about it.

"Forget everything, just tell us about the house", said Martin.

"It was the house which your great grandfather left a long time ago. It was at a village called Roslyn. They had a wine business at that time before starting gun manufacturing. It had been left abounded since then. And it is not actually a house. It is a mansion."

"Roslyn? Roslyn... I had read about it..." claimed Martin and went back to his room and checked his property papers.

"What are you looking?" asked Joyce.

"Wait a moment; I think I had read something about it, somewhere", and he found a written statement, describing a mansion and wine field and who was having the mansion's keys? "Here it is... It has been mentioned in my property papers."

"Have you gone there?" she asked.

"Never knew about this place", replied her husband.

Something struck on Joyce's mind and she insisted her husband to check that mansion. If the mansion was in good condition, then they could stay there for a while and summer vacation of Alicia was right on the way and she was in school now. Martin agreed and thought it was not a bad idea. They went back to Kevin's room and asked how far Roslyn was?

"About four hours, from here", answered Kevin.

"And how many times had you gone there?" asked Joyce.

"Hardly twice... only to meet Victor the caretaker of the mansion and it's been very long since then."

They decided to go right then and they went on a carriage to Roslyn. They reached the village; they found that it was a hilly region, surrounded by forests. They came to a village which had nineteen residents, including the village church and the surrounding was very quiet as compared to the city. The villagers who saw them passing, wondered who could be them? After crossing the village colony, they arrived on bricked road which directly led them to the gate of the mansion.

They found that the mansion gate was locked and forgot to meet the caretaker. They returned back to the village and asked the villagers about the person named Victor and one of them said that he leaves near the village church. They went to the church and found the priest and he told them that he lives in a cabin near the graveyard.

They went and found the cabin, easily. Kevin knocked the door. But nobody responded. Then he knocked even harder.

"Victor! Victor! Are you inside", he said.

Meanwhile, Joyce walked around the village streets. Village children were staring at her and when she turned to them, they run away laughing and smiling. At one of the resident, a woman was taking down the clothes from the wire which she had hanged to dry.

"Good afternoon", said Joyce.

The women heard her voice and turned.

"Good afternoon, how can I help you?" she replied, politely.

"No, no I don't need help. I was just passing by..."

"Pardon me, who are you?" coming close to the fence.

"Oh, my name is Joyce Wilkinson."

"You are a Wilkinson", she was surprised. "Well, it's been a long time since you people came to visit here."

"Actually, we never know about this place and today itself we learnt about it and we came."

"Oh... So are you the daughter... granddaughter of late Lawrence Wilkinson."

"No no, they are my in-laws. My husband Martin was their son and we have come to see the mansion. You know that mansion over there."

"Yes, yes."

"And what's your name?" asked Joyce.

"Oh, my apologies, my name is Maria."

"Well Maria, nice to meet you."

"You too, Mrs. Wilkinson", replied Maria with a smile.

"Please call me Joyce."

After several knock, Victor responded the door. He was an old man even more aged than Kevin. He looked drowsy and eyes were red and he got the smell of sweat and liquor on him.

"Are you Victor?" asked Martin to the old drunken man.

He nodded, "Yes that is me, what sort of business that brings you people", and then Victor recognized Kevin. "Hey Kevin, is that you?"

"Of course it's me. I thought you would have forgotten me."

"Come inside", said Victor.

His cabin was very dirty and liquor smell was around and also a lot of liquor filled bottles were under his bed.

"You live rubbish, Victor", commented Kevin. "You need to clean your room, at least twice a week."

"Do I look like a woman to you? Obviously not", he replied.

"Still I would prefer to clean my own room", said Kevin.

Victor laughed and took out a bottle of liquor.

"Would you like to drink kid?" he asked Martin and Kevin snatched the bottle from his hand.

"Hey, return it back, that's mine", protested Victor.

"Sorry Victor, business first", replied Kevin, polity.

"What business?"

"The person, whom you called kid is our boss", he introduced Martin to Victor. "You may not have seen him but I guess you must have heard about him. His name is Martin Wilkinson."

"Martin Wilkinson?" he captioned.

"Yes, you heard it correct and we are here to retrieve the mansion's keys."

"Oh, you must be the grandson of the wrinkled old man called Lawrence Wilkinson, right", said Victor to Martin.

"Language Victor, mind your language", insisted Kevin, in a flat rage voice.

"Why should I mind my language to the boss who doesn't pay me?"

"Doesn't pay you?" said Kevin.

"Yes, I want my money. For last few years I haven't been paid. I want five hundred pounds now if you want the mansion keys from me", he demanded. "And it is my right?"

Martin and Kevin excused from Victor and walked out from his cabin to talk.

"What money is he talking about?" asked Martin.

"The money which was paid for him for caretaking the mansion", replied Kevin, thoughtfully. "I think after master Lawrence died the money that he received must have paused and it is my mistake as I'm the person who only knew about it."

"Five hundred pounds is not a big sum of money for me but he look at him, he will spend all of them in drinking", concluded Martin.

After some moment of discussion, Kevin went back in and bargained with him. The deal stopped at fifty pounds and he agreed surprisingly without any complain. He handed over the keys which he had kept below his sleeping pillow. They also insisted him to come to the mansion as they don't know which key belongs to which lock. He agreed to come and walked out with Kevin. As Martin was about to walk out, he saw a family picture was hanged on the wall. He gazed it for a moment and then walked out. They found Joyce near the carriage and they went back to the mansion gate. Victor took the key and unlocked the gate and they walked inside. Joyce suddenly felt a strange chill under her skin and she stopped.

"Joyce, what's wrong?" asked Martin.

"...Nothing", she replied.

The mansion was two floors high and the main door was facing straight the gate. Victor unlocked the main door and opened it. They walked inside and found that there were stairs beside the door.

"Where do these stairs go to?" asked Joyce, gazing up.

"Nowhere", replied Victor. "It ends up at an empty room of the final floor. There is another stairs case from inside the living room that will lead to the upper floors."

"Why did they there is a spare stairs to an empty room?" asked Martin.

"I don't know", replied Victor.

They walked inside to the huge living room. They found that there was furniture covered under white sheets. Martin removed one and sat on it. It was in good condition. Then Victor showed them all the seven rooms of the ground floor including the bedrooms with old beds and the kitchen.

"Old furniture is still in good condition, little dusty, doors need to be oiled, plumbing should be repaired and bird house and spider webs. Rest seems to be fine", concluded Kevin, after observing the ground floor.

"It is at more good condition than I expected", said Martin.

"It seemed nice, why they abounded this mansion?" questioned Joyce.

"I heard from my grandfather that the grapes field dried and that's why they moved to the city", replied Victor.

"Your grandfather..." said Martin.

"He worked as butler, just like Kevin."

"That explains why you were given the in charge", said Kevin.

Then they went to the first floor and checked all of the room in which two rooms were bigger than the rest. One was the library with empty book shelves and the other one was a bedroom but the condition was the same as Kevin described earlier. The bedroom had a huge rectangular empty picture frame hanging on the wall. They all gazed at it.

"An empty picture frame?" commented Joyce.

"Seemed like it was the great-great grandfather Wilkinson's room", concluded Kevin.

Martin gazed out of the window. The village can be seen and then he saw electric lines coming to the villages. Suddenly, Victor felt sick and wanted to get some fresh air. He instructed them about the keys that they are arranged in a line like the rooms and they had marked numbers to which floor the keys belongs and walked out of the room.

"Will he be okay", said Joyce.

"Cannot guaranty", replied Martin. "He drinks a lot."

"I'm having the keys. I'm checking the second floor", said Joyce and walked out of the room.

"We will be behind you", replied Martin.

They both stayed for a little while checked the walls and then Martin remembered something about Victor.

"Sir, I think we also should go now and check the other rooms", suggested Kevin.

"Ah... wait, Kevin."

"What is it, sir?"

"It's about Victor; you must know him very well. Tell me something about him. I saw a family photo in his house and he looked fine and well than now. What happened to him and them?"

Kevin sighed.

"Well sir, Victor had a sad... let us say he had a sorrowful history. When he was first given the work as a caretaker of this mansion, everything was fine. But then a tragedy happened."

"What happened?"

"As far as I remember... his granddaughter she died due to... some sort of fever. Later his daughter-in-law became sick and died and then his son and then her wife."

"Oh dear, what kind of fever was that?" asked Martin, astonishingly.

"Well, I don't know much about it."

"It must be very painful for him."

"Yes and I think that is why he is drinking a lot."

Joyce reached the second floor and at the first sight, she found the first door which was left opened, slightly. She walked inside and felt the same chill like she felt when she entered through the gate. The room condition was same. She looked around and saw a showcase table. She went close and looked its condition. It seemed fine and it had four drawers. She checked it and found a dairy. She opened it and learnt that the author was someone called Francis Jones. Just then Martin and Kevin also arrived at the room and she showed it to her husband.

"From where did you found this?" asked Martin.

"From the showcase drawer", she answered.

Kevin walked around and looked the walls while Martin opened the dairy and a lot of dust fell on his hands and on his court. And on the second page, they found a dead dried flat cockroach. It was very disgusting and Martin closed the book and kept it back on the showcase.

"What happened, sir? What was that?"

"Just a dairy and it has a dead cockroach inside it", he replied.

"Never going to touch that again", said Joyce.

Then they checked the other rooms and in meanwhile, Victor walked up the stairs, which was near the main door. He stopped at the first floor, near a window and took out a small bottle of liquor. He opened the bottle's cap and as he was going to drink, he saw someone down, near the gate. A girl dressed in white, standing near the gate, staring at him and his liquor bottle slipped from his hand and broke on the ground. He recognized that girl immediately.

"Hey!" he cried and the girl ran away.

They were going to check the second room when they heard a cry of Victor which was deemed to hear it.

"Did anyone hear something?" asked Joyce.

"Yes I heard", said Martin.

"Sounds like Victor", concluded Kevin.

They all went out as they felt that something was wrong and they found him wandering outside the gate.

"Victor! What happened and who cried?" asked Kevin.

"I cried to the girl. A girl, a girl was here", he claimed, frustrated.

"What girl are you talking about?" repeated Kevin.

"A girl... If I catch her, I'm not letting her go", he said.

Kevin and his masters looked around and saw no one was around.

"I don't see anyone", said Kevin.

"Whoever was that must have gone now?" considered Martin.

Victor couldn't explain any further and he became silent.

"Are you okay, Victor?" asked Martin.

"Yes, yes, I'm okay now", he replied, calmly.

"For a moment we thought something had happened and we ran down to see", said Martin.

"Forgive me, I had and having my rough days."

Kevin sighed. "Okay sir, we have to go check the other rooms", he said.

Martin sighed. "Well Kevin, we had seen enough. No need to see the other rooms."

"Okay, Victor you heard it. You can lock it, now", said Kevin and Joyce handed him the keys.

But then Martin remembered about the wine production. "Excuse me, Victor, my ancestors used to produce wine. Is there any grapes field around here?"

When Martin was talking to Victor, Joyce thought that whoever the girl was must be a village girl and looked towards the road and the shrubs beside it. She kept on gazing when a pair of eyes blinked among the shrubs. That terrified her and stopped her breathe for a second.

"Joyce! Joyce!" said Martin at the same time and she turned him. "Come have to check the wine field too."

She looked back to the shrubs and it looked normal. She thought it must be her imagination and controlled her breath.

"Coming", she replied with a smile.

As she was about to follow them, suddenly she noticed muddy little footprints on the ground, near the gate entrance. She felt very strange because she felt that it was not here when they entered and it was smaller than hers. Then Martin called her again and she went with them, considering that it must be the shoe print of that village girl whom Victor was irritated. They went to the backyard and found that the lawn grass had grown tall and had collapsed barn where once wine was kept.

"When are you going to cut these grasses?" asked Kevin.

"No money, no care", replied Victor and they got nothing to reply.

They walked inside the grapes field and it was huge, which was left barren with some dried grapes plants. They walked around for a while and then they returned back to the gate.

"So what do you say about this? Should we start staying here", asked Martin to Joyce.

"Well, I cannot decide", she replied.

"It looks fine to me. We will stay", decided Martin, simply.

Joyce looked at the building. "Yes, we should stay. It is our property", she said, simply.

Martin and Kevin talked about the maintenance work. The mansion was in best condition and it would be better if they start the maintenance work now. But the problem was that to whom they should give the work. Kevin suggested that there was only one name that comes to his mind and that was Victor because he was here for a long time and giving him new work won't harm anyone. He went on Kevin's suggestion and he gave Victor the maintenance works which included bringing electric lines to the mansion. Victor wanted to agree on one condition that he should be paid one hundred pounds, only for himself. They bargained again and he agreed at thirty pounds to do the work because he hadn't taken care properly of the mansion like the back lawn grass and the inside of the house was still in dust. If he had done that he would have been paid the requested amount or even more.

Later he hired five workers from the village and four workers were sent from the city including two were plumbers. During the work, Martin decided to open a small stud and he instructed the workers to build a stable and after two weeks, everything was done. The Wilkinsons moved into the mansion with their servants and three horses. They were happy to move in and more excited was Alicia after seeing a huge and wide building for the first time, bigger than their previous house. Alicia became very excited to see the mansion and she ran towards the main door, holding her stuff girl doll.

"Don't run blindly Alicia or you will hurt yourself", perceived Joyce and she returned running back to her and again ran towards the door.

They were unloading the luggage from the carriage and taking it inside. They had also brought four horses along with them. Joyce was the last one to go, along with Kevin and he was also holding two rifles. As Joyce was about to enter through the gate, she saw the muddy little footprints. She was shocked and kept gazing it. She remembered that when she first came and saw it.

"What is the matter, ma'am?" asked Kevin.

"These footprints", she replied. "It is still here."

He looked and rubbed it with his feet. "Must be of a person, who walked on the mud and stood here", he concluded, simply.

Joyce remembered about the eye blink. She turned and looked to the shrubs. There was no movement.

Alicia saw the stairs near the main door and she went up to the second floor. She saw a long window, opened till floor with the panels. She gazed out straight to the skies. A fresh breeze blew over her face and she took a deep refreshing breath. She looked below and saw a girl dressed in white, came and stood near the gate. The girl gazed to her and Alicia smiled and waved her hand to her but she remained still. After standing for a few seconds the girl turned back and walked away.

"Alicia! Alicia!" said Martin, walking up to the top, searching for her.

"Oh… Alicia, don't run like that", he perceived her and looked the empty top room. Then he looked her daughter, looking out of the window. "What are you doing here?"

"Papa, there was a girl dressed in white and she turned away after looking to me", she claimed.

Martin gazed out and found no one down below.

"I don't see any girl."

"But papa I saw her, down below, near the gate", she claimed.

"Must be a village girl and I guess she had returned home, let's return to your mother."

Every luggage was kept on its respected room. And everyone got a respective room in the ground floor, except for the Wilkinson couple and the house maids- Emily and Daisy; they shared one room like in the previous house. Then Victor came and handed over the mansion's keys and the dairy to Martin. And he said that they found the dairy while working and hadn't read it because it was someone's private words. Martin placed the dairy on an empty bookshelf of his room and came out and sat on a couch. Everyone was exhausted and also hungry. Their cook James also arrived with his luggage and he cooked for them when they were in the city house.

"Oh you arrived right on time, we all are hungry", said Martin.

Without any unreasonable reply, he said, "Okay sir, show me the kitchen."

In the kitchen the raw foods and spices had already bought and kept. After thirty-five minutes James cooked delicious food and they ate it as if it was the first time they ate such a delicious meal though it was a regular meal which James cook.

"You have cooked great", greeted Joyce.

"Fantastic", said Martin and so said others.

And so the first night in the mansion passed and they all had a wonderful sleep. Next morning, Martin instructed Alicia, how to ride a horse at the back lawn while others watched them from under a shed and the old collapsed barn was turned into horse stable.

Kevin was watching them too when he heard the sobbing voice of a little girl. He looked at his Mistress and other two maids. They looked as if they heard nothing. He looked back to the mansion, when suddenly he saw a hint of something white moved away from the mansion's side. He thought it must be some mischief village children and he excused from the rest and went to catch them. There was no one at the side and then he walked to the gate and found that it was opened, slightly. He walked out and saw there was no one.

They must have run away, he thought but as he was going to return, he saw the footprints near the entrance. Just then he heard galloping sound and a carriage arrived. It stopped by him and Donald the manager of Martin stepped out.

"Mr. Donald, what brings you here?" he asked.

"I want to meet, Mr. Wilkinson, Kevin", he replied.

Kevin introduced him to Martin. And he served them tea and snacks.

"Sir, I'm here to tell you that I found a house and guess you got already one", he said.

"Sorry for the trouble. I forgot to tell you, I already, got another home", replied Martin.

"It is huge and beautiful, when did you buy it?"

"No, I didn't buy it. It was with my family for very long, they were wine producers before changing their profession to gun sellers."

"It's nice and I liked this place. It is very peaceful than the city noise."

"Yes, you are right. It is peaceful."

"And by the way, I had to inform two more things. First was that inspector Turner had come to me and he told me that he wanted to meet you and also the architecture man? He told me that you wanted to rebuild your city house that was burnt down."

"Yes, I want to build back my house but I had told him that, once the investigation is over then I will allow him."

"Oh, I will remind him again and don't forget to meet Inspector Turner. He wanted to meet you after two days from now."

"Okay, I will and I will."

"Okay sir", said Donald and after a while he left.

Later when they were having lunch, Joyce suggested Martin that they should through a party and invite all the villagers to make a good relationship with them. Martin thought about it and it was not a bad idea and asked when they should through the party.

"After two days", she said. "On Saturday and everyone will be free in the evening."

"No, it cannot be happening. We should look another day."

"But why? And it will be late."

"I have to meet Inspector Turner and the architecture about rebuilding the former house. I won't be available to help."

"Then don't worry, Kevin, James and I will handle it, including making the invitation cards. James had told that he will look after the food and Kevin and I will look after the invitation."

"Okay then, I will look after the expense", he said.

Next day Martin went for work to his factory for the employee payday and on the other hand, the preparation for the party started. Kevin also went to the city and made thirty invitation venerable cards from the card maker while James collected all the food supplies and wine. By the evening, everything was gathered for the party. That evening all the servants walked around the mansion and then they walked upstairs which was near the entrance.

"This place is amazing, isn't it James?" said Daisy, joyfully.

"Yes indeed but I'm a village boy and this is not a new thing for me", he replied.

Then Emily went close to the window and gazed out. The village can be seen completely including the field, the church and the graveyard. She gazed down and saw a girl dressed in white, standing near the gate. Daisy joined her and gazed to the village.

"Who is that girl?" said Emily.

"Who?" asked Daisy.

"There below, near the gate", pointed Emily.

Daisy looked below and saw the girl. She was staring up at them.

Both the maids felt strange, and then Kevin also joined them at the window and saw that girl.

"Who is she?" he questioned.

James also got interested and wanted to see that girl but till then the girl had walked away.

"Must be a village girl", guessed Kevin.

"But what was she doing here?" said Daisy.

The following day they distributed all the invitation cards to each and respective houses. Joyce went to Maria's house to invite her with her daughter and found three other women in her house. They both were delighted to meet each other again and Maria introduced Joyce to her friends and their children.

Tory and her two sons Adam and Rupert, Emma and her daughter Flora, and Lily and her twin sons Joseph and Joshua and finally she introduced her own daughter Julia and then all of them were introduced to Alicia. They were the same children who ran away smiling when Joyce first came to the village. After the introduction and little talk with them, Joyce gave the invitation card to each of the ladies. They all were neighbours and Joyce requested them not to forget to come for the party, tomorrow evening. Then Julia requested her that she wanted to see and explore the mansion from inside.

"Sure, come anytime when you want", permitted Joyce, smiling.

"Can I come too? Sound's childish but I also… wanted to see the mansion from the inside", requested Tory.

"Sure why not, all of you came now then", said Joyce, happily, as she wanted to make more friends and also for her daughter.

But Alicia had made friends with them before she thought of it. Maria left a note for her husband that they are going to Wilkinson's mansion and then they went. Joyce became their guide and showed them the lawn, old grapes field and all the floor of the building. As they were walking out of the main door, Tory noticed the stairs going up and asked about it. Joyce also doesn't know, what was up there and so they all walked up while the children went to the lawn. They walked up and found an empty room and window facing to the village.

"What is this floor for", asked Emma.

"I haven't been here", replied Joyce.

"Does someone live here?" said Lily.

"I think they were trying to make… a store room", guessed Maria.

"I can see the whole village", said Tory and they all looked one by one through the window.

"Mrs. Wilkinson… can I ask you something", said Lily.

"You are free to ask what ever and call me Joyce", she said.

"Why did you move here?"

Joyce smiley face turned pale. "Sorry, if the reason is personal then, then I'm sorry…"

"Nothing personal actually", replied Joyce. "I was actually our house caught fire and I and my daughter and everyone else survived barely."

"Oh God", said Emma, shocked.

"Was someone hurt?" asked Maria.

"No, no one was hurt, everyone ran out before the damage", she replied and the ladies felt relieved.

"This is tragic..." commented Emma.

"Yes it is... okay ladies, we are done here, let's go down", said Joyce and they started walking down.

As they reached to the first-floor window, Maria saw something through the window. She stopped and peeked out down. She saw a girl dressed in white, standing outside.

"Who is that girl?"

"What are you looking?" asked Tory and joined her and then Emma and Lily.

Joyce had walked down and when she walked back to join them, the girl had already gone. The ladies thought she must be Cobb's daughter Brea and ignored. They walked down and Maria thanked Joyce that her daughter wishes came true and so do other children wishes because they always wanted to get inside the mansion and play.

The following day Martin went to the city again to meet Inspector Turner and he told him that they had the investigation was complete a week ago and forgot to inform because he was assigned to a murder case. The murder case was also closed and now he got the time to inform him. He explained that during the search, they found nothing reasonable that the cause of the fire was done on purpose rather they considered that it may have happened because of some carelessness. Martin trusted his investigation because he was also thinking the same. Then he signed a statement and went to the architecture. He gave him the permission to rebuild his house. In the evening, when he returned back, everything was ready for the party. He quickly became fresh and the party started. The party went splendid and everybody enjoyed it eating, drinking and dancing. Before nine o'clock, all the guests returned home.

When the last guest went Kevin was going to close the gate when he noticed the muddy little footprints again. It was still near the gate entrance. He was stunned and he first thought it might be the footprint of one of the guests and then he remembered about the girl whom he saw from the top, yesterday. That was the first time; he felt something strange was happening around and the footprint was on the exact same place like... he had seen when they came to live for the first time. He closed the gate and went back inside but he didn't notice Victor was sitting beside the gate. Victor took out a bottle of liquor and started to drink and he then fell asleep. It was a full moon night and also the gate had the light bulbs. Some noise broke his sleep and he was awake. He yawned and suddenly he saw the girl dressed in white and her hands were bloody red, standing near the gate and staring to the mansion like always.

"Hey!" he cried and stood up.

The girl ran and he ran after her. He chased her to the graveyard and accidentally he slipped and fell and knocked his head on a gravestone. After a few moments, he woke up with severe pain on the head and he was walked to his cabin. On the way, he fell into an open grave. He stood up and learnt that the grave was not deep. He could easily climb out on his beer hands. As he placed his hand on the surface something grabbed his right leg and started to pull him. He resisted it but then more hands came out from the walls of the grave and pulled him into. The hands were the corpse of his family. The girl dressed in white appeared on the surface with a shovel and started to put dust on him. He tried to scream out but one of the corpse limbs grabbed his lips.

"Victor! Victor! Wake up", said the priest and he woke up and he was shocked that he was fine but still had pain on his head.

"What? Drinking a lot", said the priest.

He paused for long.

"Victor..." said the priest.

"No father no, I just was coming and fell on the rock and… I was unconscious", he replied, little confused about the dream.

The priest sighed. "Okay, see you later, help yourself", he said and went back to the church.

Victor stood up and went into his cabin and sat on the bed. He looked at the picture of his late family. He stood up to drink some water but suddenly he felt pain on his right leg. He pulled his pants up and found a hand mark on his leg. Then, he found another hand mark was on his wrist, and also in both of his arms and he took off his shirt and found there were all on his body. He got scared and took another fresh bottle of liquor and started to drink.

Next day, Alicia complained of her missing doll. Her mother suggested that they will look for it when they come back from the church. They went to the church and it was Wilkinson's first church day at Roslyn and they all went to attend the mass. Just between the mass Julia, Maria's daughter started to cough, later it became so bad that she and her husband, had to leave. After the mass Martin and Alicia went home because Alicia was still complaining about her doll while Joyce went to Maria's house to have a visited. She found that Julia was in very bad condition. She was coughing blood and had a very high fever and her father had gone to call the doctor from the nearby village.

"Have you eaten anything?" asked Joyce.

"Yes, we had", replied Maria, worried.

"Okay I'll be back", said Joyce and went to the mansion.

She gathered some fruits in a basket and went back to Maria's house and gave it to her so that they will eat later. She had stopped coughing and then again she started coughing and her face had turned pale. Soon Maria's husband arrived with the doctor and he checked her condition. Then he gave Julia a medicine in which her coughing stopped and she felt little rest.

"How long is she sick?" asked the doctor.

"From today", replied Maria.

"Today, but her condition shows that she was sick for a week", he replied.

"They are telling you the truth, their daughter was sick since this morning", supported Joyce.

"But she doesn't like she is sick today."

Then the doctor gave them some tablets and instructed to fetch her whenever she starts coughing and when the medicine was finished, he asked to come and get more from him and then he took his payment. As the doctor was about to leave on his horse, a person from the neighbourhood came running to him. It was Tory's husband. He stopped the doctor and requested him to look treat his son.

Joyce excused from Maria and started to walk home. She was passing by Tory's house, she found Rupert sitting near the door.

"Hello Rupert... is everything alright?" she asked and the boy shakes his head, no. He was very upset for his brother, Adam.

Then a rattling noise came from inside.

"Be careful!" "I'm careful!"

Joyce walked inside the house and saw Adam had the same condition as Julia. She was stunned because he was okay this morning at the church. Tory saw Joyce and she came to her and said, "Please, Mrs Wilkinson... now is not the good time. Leave us now."

She walked out and Rupert was called inside. Joyce felt something strange about the fever that these two children were suffering and walked back to her mansion. She talked about it with Martin and he recommended that not to worry about them. It must be coincident that they are suffering a common fever and they will be fine in few days.

Next morning, they got a sad message from a fellow villager that both the children had died and there funeral was at mid-noon. It shocked Joyce and she felt very sorry for their loss. Julia's and Adam's family grieved for them. After a ceremonial prayer, they were buried at the cemetery. On the same day, Tory's other son, Rupert, Emma's daughter, Flora and Lily's twin son Joseph and Joshua became sick like Julia and Adam. The village doctor came and couldn't save them. They also died that night and on the next day, they were taken for burial. All of them were present and Joyce was gazing the open grave. Suddenly she saw eyes blinked from the mud. She got scared and closed her eyes. Her husband thought she must be feeling sad for those kids. He patted on her hand. When she opened her eyes, they had started put down the coffin.

They all returned back to their respective houses. It was a very sorrowful day for everyone. After this, it made some villagers believe that something was not right, something was killing their children. During the lunch, Joyce ate nothing and walked out of the gate to make up her mind. Suddenly, she heard noises from the shrubs, beside the road. She looked to it and the wind started to blow. She kept on gazing the shrubs and eyes blinked again. She got scared and she ran into the mansion. Later all of them came with her holding rifles and search the person, among the shrubs.

"Are you sure, there was a person?" asked Martin. "Not a stray dog."

"And if a person like a small kid would be hiding here then, then the shrubs would have been bent", said James.

"I'm sure! Someone was watching me or something is watching me since the first time when we got here!"

"Then why didn't you told this earlier?" asked Martin.

"I thought, it was just my imagination but now I'm sure that there is something watching."

"Something? Are you trying to say you saw a ghost, ma'am?" considered James.

"Yes something like that..." she answered, frustrated.

Then she remembered about the muddy little footprints and it was still there.

Kevin was amazed and he admitted that he had seen it two times. Martin bowed and picked a pinch of mud. It was still wet and he looked to the off-road mud. He checked the mud and found that they both have different colours.

"What is it sir?" asked James.

"It is wet and the off road mud doesn't match with this one. Looks like someone was definitely here or he or she is coming always", considered Martin.

"It must be her", said Emily.

"What are you talking about?" asked Martin.

"Don't you remember that day, James when we were on that stairs and we saw that girl?"

"Which girl? I don't remember", replied James.

"The girl we saw, when we peeked out from the window, from there", pointing the second floor.

"But, I don't remember any girl that I had seen."

"Yes, yes, I do", interrupted Kevin. "I was there when I saw that girl."

When they were searching and talking, Daisy was cleaning the dishes, when she heard the sobbing voice of a girl. She thought it was Alicia must be playing and she might have hurt herself and went to see her.

"Alicia!" she said and heard her sobbing voice again, coming from the boundary of barren grapes field where they had stable.

She heard her voice again and went to see her by herself. She walked into the boundary and looked around. There was no one in the field and neither around the stable expect for the three horses. She thought she must be hearing something else and as she turned to return, she heard her sobbing voice again. This time it was no mistake that she was not imagining. She felt something moved to her right side and turned. She saw something moving on the ground. She went close to it and saw it some kind of rolled dirty cloth and touched it with her right feet.

Suddenly it rose up. It was a human hand that came out of the ground. It shocked and terrified Daisy and she fell back. The hand caught her feet and Daisy screamed for help and the horses neighed. She struggled and looses the sandal to get free from the grip. She stood up, sobbing and ran away with terror.

Meantime Kevin said, "...I thought she was a village girl."

"Village girl?" said Martin. "How does she look like?"

"Never got to see her properly but and it was the only time, when I, Daisy and Emily, saw her from the top floor."

Daisy came running and terrified and fell near on the way to the entrance. It surprised them and they ran to pick her.

"What happened?" asked James.

"Someone thing was there in the backfield, something, a hand grabbed my feet", she said, sobbing.

"What were you doing there?" asked James, astonished.

"I thought, it was Alicia", she replied.

Alicia was not there, they got terrified but then Martin saw her daughter. She was on the first floor and gazing down to them and then everyone noticed. Martin went up and asked her policy, "Alicia what are you doing here?"

"I'm waiting for someone."

"Waiting for whom?"

"A girl, she always stands near the gate and gazes to me but whenever I run to the gate, she was gone."

Martin looked to the gate and then to her daughter. "For how long you are seeing here?"

She turned to him and said, "Since we got here?"

He caught her hand and said that mummy must be looking for her and took her down.

"Is everything okay, sir?" asked Kevin, in a low voice.

He shook his head no.

Then they went back to the stud and looked that place. Daisy showed that place and stood at a distance with her Mistress. They found Daisy's sandal and near it, the ground was dug. Martin felt something suspicious and asked Kevin to bring a shovel. He brought and he dug it. There was nothing under the ground except the mud. But then Martin noticed the colour of the mud which they dug out looked similar to which the footprints was made near the gate. The horses neighed and one of them tapped legs and then they got calm. Martin understood, it meant that someone else was here. They returned back, sat in the living room.

"I think this mansion is haunted by ghosts", considered Daisy.

"But I didn't experience anything strange", said James.

"Neither me", said Martin.

"Me neither", said Emily.

"Forget everything... I don't know why you all didn't experience, but I do and now Daisy... and if you think it was not done by a spirit, then where is that person and why is he scaring us?" said Joyce.

They remained silently for a while.

"I think I have an explanation", said Martin. "It's been almost more than one week and anything strange you both had experienced had happened outside the house, not inside."

"So what shall we do now, sir? Shall we live now?" asked James, little terrified.

"I guess we should.... but let's just don't rush...." said Martin.

"Oh very great", complimented Joyce.

"Then what are you going to do, sir?" asked Daisy. "I'm scared and I don't want to be here."

"I'll talk to Victor. He was the caretaker right. He must know something. He should have told us if something was not right? And as far as I remember he was also complaining about a girl when we first came to check the mansion."

"Then we should go now ask him first", suggested Kevin.

Martin and Kevin went to meet while others stayed at home. He was not at home. They asked the priest and other villagers but they did not know where he went? They returned as it was getting dark. They couldn't go back to the city because they had to pass through a forest road and it was not safe during the night.

Next morning a relative of Kevin and Emily arrived at the same time. They informed them that Kevin's granddaughter and Emily's son had died of fever. It shocked everyone; two deaths message at the same time. Kevin and Emily sobbed and their masters felt very sorry for them. They went to the city with them for the funeral.

Then the rest also decided to go but Martin also wanted to know, what was going on. He went back to meet Victor and he was still not at home. Then he remembered about the girl, who always come and stand near the gate which his servant and his daughter were speaking about.

Martin walked up to the first floor of the front stairs to see the girl, call her and ask her questions. He also took his gun with him if possible of danger. Meanwhile, Joyce and the rest were packing everyone's clothes from their room. She brought a briefcase and placed it on the living and went to bring another when she noticed the dairy kept on the empty bookshelf. She picked it up and went to her room to pack it. The dead cockroach was not in it and she started to read.

The dairy belonged to a person called Francis Jones not to a Wilkinson and his name was written inside the dairy. He described himself as a butler of Noah Wilkinson, who was Martin's great-great grandfather. She read word for word of the first page and then the second page and continued reading. The writer had described his relationship, marriage and his two children named Ian and Malcolm and the good manners of his master Noah Wilkinson towards him and the villagers and the flourishing wine business.

As she was about to turn another page, the dairy slipped from her hand and fell on the ground. The dairy landed opened. She picked it up and started reading again from the opened page. It had addressed the children of Noah. Son's name was William Wilkinson and younger daughter's name was Anna Wilkinson. Anna was ten years old when she received her first Holy communion and all the family along with relatives and villagers came to the mansion to celebrate but the night after the party she became sick. The village doctors were called and they tried to cure her but all of them failed. After two days as she was going to be taken to the city, she died near the gate and was buried at the village cemetery.

She continued reading. Jones writes, 'After one month of her death. The villagers who worked in the mansion claimed that they saw someone like Anna standing near the gate. Then many of them started to see. Even I saw her from the first floor but the master and her family didn't. I had also seen her but when I was going to tell it about I found my master became angry on those who claimed to see her and so I remained silent. Later after four days, the younger children of the servants started to become sick and then died. The fever was just the same as what Anna was suffering. She had become pale and she was coughing out blood, regularly. Then my younger son Malcolm also become sick and died. It was a big painful day for me and my wife. I remained, sitting near the son's grave in agony for a day. But when I was about to return I heard the cry of my late son from below...' Then there were no more sentences.

When she didn't arrive after waiting for two hours, Martin thought he was wasting time and as he was going to walk down the girl dressed in white-red dress showed up near the gate and she started to stare him. Martin was shocked and then he gazed to her dress and noticed that it was not the red colour, it was the blood on her dress and on her hands and she was holding Alicia's doll. Joyce felt strange after reading the dairy and walked to the window and she also saw the girl standing near the gate. Martin ran quickly outside to catch her and Joyce saw her walking away and then Martin running after her. He ran till the village but the girl vanished into the thin air. Joyce got very terrified. She considered that the girl was Anna Wilkinson.

When Martin returned, she showed him the dairy. There was no doubt that it was the ghost of Anna Wilkinson and was the daughter of Noah Wilkinson. Then Martin remembered about the personal album of his grandfather. He took out it from the briefcase and looked all the photos. He recognised Anna, in the photo and she was dressed in her communion dress. Some of the photos were from the First communion party of Anna and all other relatives were present. Daisy also recognised seeing that girl.

Joyce and Martin went to the village and found Maria, Tory, Emma and Lily and their husbands gathering on the street, including other villagers. The villagers told them that something satanic was going on here and the Wilkinson told that them that they just discovered that what was going on and who might be doing it. They showed the photo of Anna and the ladies recognised that girl, seeing through the mansion's window first floor and she considered that those who see her, their children dies and they saw her recently.

At the same moment, they realized that they both had also seen her and James came running to search them and told them that Alicia had become suddenly sick. They ran back and it stunned Joyce and Martin. She was coughing blood and her face had turned pale, just like the daughter of Maria. James quickly brought the carriage and they sat and rode towards the city. They admitted her in a hospital and her treatment started but before the midnight Alicia died. Her parents sobbed very hard and it was very hard for them to resist it and on the next day they buried her at the city cemetery, next to his grandfather Lawrence.

By the following, the sad couple along with Daisy and James returned back to the mansion and found Alicia's doll near the entrance. Joyce sobbed, holding it and Martin hugged her. Then they went inside and packed the remaining and set to leave. Before leaving they called a village meeting in the church and explained everything, what happened and they were the victim too. They all felt sympathy for each other and the priest said that he will pray for the demonic soul to leave earth. Then the Wilkinsons got into the carriages and started to return home and left the horses in the villager. Joyce saw her friends and they waved their hands and she waved them back. It was the saddest moments in all of their life while will haunt them till their own death. As they came out of the village road to the forest road a dirty man came in front of them. It was Victor. It amazed them and Martin got off the carriage and grabbed his collar in anger.

"Victor where were you when we needed you?" he burst on him.

"I tried to warn everyone but nobody listened", he replied.

"Don't hurt him", said Joyce and he left his collar and Victor falls on the ground.

"Let's go now", said Joyce coming to him and pulled him into the carriage. The carriage passed by him.

"You can still save your daughter now if you want!" he cried.

They stopped the carriage and Martin came out and asked him how?

"My grandfather name was Francis Jones. He told me how his younger son died and the rest of the people who saw Anna's ghost. When my grandfather was near the grave of my younger brother he heard his cry from the coffin as if they were alive. He took a shovel and tried to dig but people caught him and took him jail. He warned us, me if anyone who sees her, the youngest member of the family dies alive. But I didn't listen and I lost my family", explained Victor, sobbing.

"Why would Anna's ghost be killing our children? She died of fever", asked Joyce.

"Because she was buried alive, by accident and that's why she is killing", answered Victor. "Hurry up your daughter must be alive now in the coffin."

Martin said nothing and took a horse out of the carriage and rode as fast as he could.

He reached the city cemetery and found a shovel easily, kept near a tree by a grave digger. He started to dig Alicia's grave and almost dug till her coffin. He kept digging, until he was very tired. He was taking a breath when she heard the cry of her daughter.

"Papa! help me! help me!"

"Alicia! Hold on!" he said and he continued digging again.

Two grave keepers saw him digging and they came and pulled him away from the grave. Martin found them with all his strength and hit one of them with the shovel. The other one caught him from back and Martin struggled. A policeman was passing by and he saw them fighting. Martin somehow set loose from his grip and pushed him down. The policeman came running, blowing his whistle. Martin was so frustrated to save her daughter that he forgot what he was doing? He took out his gun and shot both the grave diggers. The policeman was shocked and took out his own gun and asked him to surrender or he will shot him. But Martin didn't listen and pulled the trigger. They shot each other dead.

- Charles E. Ekka

www.ingramcontent.com/pod-product-compliance
Lightning Source LLC
Chambersburg PA
CBHW030533130626
46552CB00006B/2237